CREATED TO SOAR

BY HS JACKSON

Cover Design by Becky Blanton - beckyblanton.com
Editing by Becky Blanton - beckyblanton.com

ISBN: 978-1-7368253-1-0

DEDICATION

This book was inspired by my husband, David Jackson, who is my partner and best friend. He is my sounding board and always has words of encouragement. I can look to him to provide me a different perspective and with insight.

I will always remember his advice on one particular day when I felt totally discouraged about my day.

He said, "No you had a bad moment, that you allowed to control your entire day." I thank God for gifting me this talent to be an author. My mission is to add value to others, partnering with them to see that there is another and better way. Do not allow our environment or others to control who and what we can become. Believe in that which is within you and to whom you belong.

*"But those who hope in the LORD
will renew their strength. They will soar
on wings like eagles; they will run and not
grow weary, they will walk and not be faint."*

~ Isaiah 40:31

INTRODUCTION

[Unless otherwise indicated, all Bible quotes are from the New International Version (NIV) Bible.]

Created to Soar is the third book I have written. My two other books were *Reflections from Within* and *Messages from Spirit.* Both were daily word books designed to provide you with an inspiring nugget to launch your day, or to provide you with a nudge to continue pressing forward during your day.

Created to Soar is designed to provide you with the parts of my story that inspired me to write. Know that God created us to soar, not to just coast along, but to be significant and impactful. We are to spread our wings and fly. Aspiring to soar higher each day of our life, reaching new plateaus is part of God's will for us. Each day strive to focus on, what can you do to add value to yourself and the others in your community? Life is a journey. Enjoy it and embrace it.

The Apostle Paul says it best:

"However, I consider my life worth nothing to me; my only aim is to finish the race and complete the task the Lord Jesus has given me — the task of testifying to the good news of God's grace." ~Acts 20:24.

Paul was headed to Jerusalem. He knew that he was going to face unimaginable hardship and pain. He met with the disciples to say good-bye, knowing that he would never see them again. He told them that he was compelled by the Spirit to do God's will.

This is the same task for all of us — to do God's will. God created each of us for His purpose. He has implanted gifts within us to be used in this world to glorify and edify Him.

"In him we were also chosen, having been predestined according to the plan of him who works out everything in conformity with the purpose of his will." ~ Ephesians 1:11.

Each of us has been created by God and appointed a place where we will be called to duty. We are to accept God's appointment so that we travel along the road which I call our journey. We are to enjoy our journey, so that we live boldly, having no regrets.

Even when it's challenging and difficult, there should be no regrets. Why? Because all that happens along the journey is adding to your character.

God is molding you into a person who can withstand pain and hardship. Along this path you are gaining wisdom and becoming conscious of the gifts within you that will enable you to tap into and release your potential. Potential is our gift from God.

Have you ever undertaken a health or walking program? Did you notice you couldn't get very far that first day of walking? However, if you kept it up, each day you could walk a little farther. You were building up your endurance. Yes, it was uncomfortable. You may have gotten winded, or your muscles and legs hurt.

But in the end, you became fitter and healthier! God is doing the same thing with our character and our spirit. Every challenge along the way is designed to strengthen us. He has a plan, trust me. He does.

We will not live in this world forever, thus it is imperative that we embrace our cause and run the race for which we have been predestined. Our goal is to finish well. You and I do not wish to look back with regrets having allowed opportunities and possibilities to be missed, not acted upon. Recall the *Parable of the Bags of Gold*, Matthew 25:14-30.

The master gave each servant a bag of gold with which to invest or use as he saw fit. Every servant but one was able to earn more with the gold he was given, except for the one servant who chose to do nothing with the bag of gold he had been gifted. This angered the master and resulted in his bag of gold being taken away and given to another who had done something with his gift. For us the bag of gold represents the talents we have been gifted. If we do not use what has been gifted, it will be taken away and given to another. God created us to soar, so we are to be bold like an eagle. Did you know that eagles are the only birds who love a storm? All other birds try to hide, to seek protection, or to flee from storms. Not the eagle.

Eagles will fly into the fierceness of a storm and use the wind of the storm to rise higher to get above the chaos — often in just a matter of seconds.

When storms arise, we are to do the same, soaring to higher ground and becoming better and stronger, not intimidated by the storm, but emboldened by it. We are to rise above it and soar over the turmoil below us.

During our life journey, we will encounter trials and storms that we must embrace, adding to our character. We are challenged with evolving, growing and transforming to become impactful and exceptional.

We are bound to fulfill the purpose for our existence. Know that we are blessed to have a road that does have obstacles because obstacles allow us to see the unlimited possibilities and potential God has for us.

Obstacles lead to growing and learning. They allow us to fail, and failures empower us to press forward to success.

The road we travel will sometimes be unpaved and rocky because these are the paths to the lessons that must be learned. I call these invaluable lessons—lessons that will build resilience.

During the times of trials, ensure time is taken to pause and reflect on what is happening, otherwise the lessons will be lost. Lessons are only invaluable if time is taken to evaluate, pause and reflect. Applying the information to your life, not just suffering through it, is how we grow.

In the Parable of the Lost Son, Luke 15: 11-32, the youngest son lost all his father gave him in order for him to become better. There may be a time that you lose all that you have.

Know that this loss, or these losses, may be necessary for you to reach for what is better. You must desire to have a better life. In life, we reach plateaus where we need to go further to embrace what is beyond.

This book is designed to equip you with determination which leads to being consistent and persistent as you undergo the journey of your life. By keeping your focus on God all things are possible.

It is our responsibility to uncover our possibilities and to seize the opportunities that will lead to our being impactful and significant.

It's when we learn from our trials that we can have the biggest impact and add value to this world and to others around us.

In your trials and storms, look to the One who is able to do all things, the Father. You can and will become who you have been predestined to be.

God will provide you with all that you need, and more, for you to complete your journey. I challenge you to soar as you are equipped to do.

CHAPTER ONE

Creation | The Beginning

G od said, "Let us make mankind in our image, in our likeness, so that they may rule over the fish in the sea and birds in the sky, over the livestock and all the wild animals, and over all the creatures that move along the ground.' God created mankind in his own image, in the image of God, he created them; male and female he created them." ~Genesis 1:26-27

Look at the "us," in the scripture above. This word in itself means that we are complex, not composed of just one entity. God has gifted us with His Spirit, His breath and His light. We have intellect, emotion and free will. All this is packaged in a body that I call the "shell." Man was mere dust in which life was bestowed by God breathing life into the body.

"From whence dust we were created to dust we shall return."
~ Genesis 3:19.

God has equipped us with everything that we need. Our talents are gifts in which we are the stewards. We are given these gifts in this world to put to use building up God's kingdom.

Our goal is to glorify and edify the Lord, which is the underlying purpose of our creation. We are stewards of the gifts because we are not entitled to them, but have been blessed to receive. We are to use our gifts to join God in the work He is doing.

God is always at work, and we should always be about His work. We should yearn to be invited to join God in the work that He is doing, ultimately seeking to hear the words, *well done, my faithful servant."*

We are to serve God, building communities that add value to one another, enabling us to all grow and thrive. Jesus said when you serve others you are serving Him. God has gifted us with The Spirit so that we can serve and be of service to Him. The Spirit will guide us along the path to where we need to go so that we fulfill the purpose for our creation.

Talents, Time, and Treasures

God tasks us to be a servant where we are to build up His kingdom. Being a servant requires humility, and not being self-centered. We are His children and we have all been created in the image of God.

This means that God is multicultural and diverse. He has gifted each of us with talents, time and treasures that are to be used to build up His kingdom and to glorify the Lord.

No one person is better than another because we each have been given what we need to be of service. We are given according to what God knows we can accomplish and withstand. Just as the body has hands, feet, eyes, and ears, and each plays a part in the body, we have our own unique talents that allow us to be used exactly as God intends. If you're a foot, don't be wishing you were a hand. God knows exactly what He is doing when he gives us the talents and gifts.

It is very disheartening to see how this world has supported and condoned the mindset of superiority and segregation. The world has taken being a servant out of context.

God never created man to be over another man or to be in bondage to another. What God does ask of each of us to be humble and not self-seeking. Being humble is vital in serving and being God's instrument. To be humble requires not being prideful.

"Jesus became poor so that each of us could become rich."
~ 2 Corinthians 8:9.

Jesus is our example and our incentive for genuine Christian generosity. Jesus, who is God, submitted to the humiliation of becoming a man. Humiliation in humans is hard because we seek to be superior.

The flesh is in control instead of the Spirit. When we are humble, we are honoring and serving God. Serving should be our top goal and priority.

"We should do nothing out of selfish ambition or vain conceit. Rather in humiliation value others above yourselves, not looking to your own interests but each of you to the interests of the others." – Philippians 2:4-5.

Jesus said, "I did not come to be served, but to serve." Matthew 20:28. He also said, "The one who loves his life will lose it, and the one who hates his life in this world will keep it for eternal life." ~ John 12:25.

Thus, we are to live a life of serving in the name of the Lord. If we do so, then we will be rewarded in this life and the life that is to come. We must seek to emulate Jesus, serving Him and seeking to be with Him forever. We have to say no to our selfishness and pride.

We cannot live a life that is focused on self, but instead we should focus on being a servant to others. Our reward is not the things of this world, but in the life that is to come. We need to strive to be like Jesus, who humbled himself. He suffered humiliation for each of us so we could become rich in spirit — not in material things.

Our mission is to live a life of service. Jesus washed the feet of his disciples. He did this to show that nothing was beneath Him. *He* did not believe He was greater or better than anyone, and He was God. Jesus, through his actions, shows us the way that we are to live and be of service.

It is okay to get dirty and have to roll up your sleeves. If we are to please God and use our gifts and talents, we must get in the trenches—helping others who are in need, hurting or suffering. It is our call to duty using the talents, time and treasures we have been provided.

God shows us that no one race is dominant or has dominion over another. Only God has dominion over man, so do not bow and cower to man when God is the one we should be concerned with pleasing and following. Each of us are tasked with having power and dominion. You were created to rule over God's creation. You are a king or queen irrespective of what others think or believe of you.

In Genesis 1:28, God blessed them and said to them:

"Be fruitful and increase in number; fill the earth and subdue it."

God tasks each of us with filing this world with His people through procreation. God's plan is that we serve one another to become better.

By not believing in yourself, you place limits on God, who is limitless. You have all within you and with you to become exceptional. Take control of your mind. You must think positively about who you are and keep your focus on who you can become. Fill your mind with what can be instead of what is. Positive thoughts and thinking will enable you to focus your energy on positive actions leading to accomplishment and fulfillment.

"As a man thinketh so he shall be." ~ *Proverbs 23:7.*

You are beautiful. Stop looking to man for approval and instead look within yourself and to God. Treat yourself as the royalty to which you are entitled. You and I are heirs of God, thus claim your inheritance.

The Spirit

We have the gift of the Holy Spirit, the Spirit of truth. The Spirit renews our hearts. He is our guidance counselor who fuels us with light and life. The Spirit is our Advocate in this world. The Spirit will convict us when we make decisions that are against the Word of God and it will provide correction. God has provided us with the power of choice which is our will; however, we must choose wisely. In Deuteronomy 30, God offered us life or death.

"See, I set before you today life and prosperity, death and destruction."
~ *Deuteronomy 30:15.*

Choose life, loving the Lord with all your heart, mind, soul and spirit. Follow His commands, His decrees, and His laws. If you do these things, God will bless you abundantly.

Your life will be overflowing with all that He wants to give you. Jesus sacrificed his life for each of us to the point of humbling Himself on a cross. He was innocent, and free of sin, yet he bore our sin. He paid the price for us, gifting us with grace and mercy.

Because of Adam and Eve, sin entered the world. Because of God's unconditional love for us, He made a new covenant, gifting us with salvation through our Savior, Jesus. Jesus is the light of this world and the bread of life. Jesus after his sacrifice, returned to the Father so the Father would send the Spirit to each of us as a gift.

Jesus said to the disciples, "I have to go but the Father will gift you with the Holy Spirit." ~ John 15:26.

The Spirit was sent by the Father and the Son to infuse us with light and truth. It holds us accountable to God and His Word. It is the application of God's salvation that equips us to do God's will. Because of the Spirit, we have within us the presence of God. The gift of grace and the Spirit is not to be wasted.

Let us not squander what we have been provided by minimizing the importance of what we have within. Lean into the Spirit, allow Him to work within your heart governing your mind, body and soul.

Wisdom

With the Spirit, we have discernment, which I call God blessing us with his wisdom. Discernment is used to make the right choices applying God's Word, using it to teach and guide us along the journey of our life. The Spirit equips us with wings so that we may soar like an eagle flying above the storms in our life. We are overcomers.

This speaks to us being creative and innovative because we seek to please God, glorifying and honoring Him. With the clarity of your why, you will live in your purpose, implementing and executing plans to draw closer to God. You will join God in the work that He is doing.

As you take action, consider your choices at the forefront doing God's will and following His Word.

Your choices must be a reflection of your obedience.

Initially, Adam and Eve were blessed with having to not perform any manual or hard labor. God supplied and provided for all of their needs. They only had to oversee the garden because God had given them dominion over all other forms of His creation.

However, Eve and Adam allowed the serpent (the Devil) to entice them into thinking they could be equal to God. That thought did not come out of their hearts. The Devil planted the seed of sin and evil while Adam and Eve provided the water for sin to grow and infiltrate this world.

Being in the image of God was not sufficient to keep them safe from the Devil. Like the fallen angels before them, they sought to become *like* God, which is never possible for any human, or any created being.

Then there is Job. He truly suffered, losing his children, property and more and all in one day! I love God's response to Job, who had the audacity to finally question Him on why he was suffering, having lost all he had been given.

God said, "Brace yourself like a man, let me question you and you shall answer me." God asked Job where he was when He created the world. Job was speechless, he could not answer. Like Adam and Eve, how could anyone ever think to be like God, or understand His ways? He, who is the Creator of all things?

As you journey through your life, there will be many times that you will be distracted and distressed by the flesh. You must hold firmly to God's word, His laws, and His spirit so that you'll be able to stand strong and firm.

In your times of weakness, pray and recite God's Word. Seek His counsel and ask Him to cover you with his wings.

Rejoice in who you are. You are God's child. Give God praise. You are created in God's image. You lack nothing. God knows what you need before you do, and He provides exactly what is needed; thus, submit your request to him and remain obedient.

There is no need to focus on "getting power" because we have something better — access to the greatest power, God. He is Almighty. He is also a jealous God, and does not like pride nor greed. Greed is what caused God to become angry and discontent with mankind, eradicating mankind from the world by flooding the entire land.

The only survivor was Noah, his family and selected animals. Noah and his family were the only ones God could find that were righteous and good. However, God regretted his actions, because of His love, grace and mercy.

He promised that never again would He rid the world of mankind. However, sin is still in the world. To address that, God established a new covenant with his children using Jesus as the conduit to provide a way for man's salvation.

The entrance of sin does not change that you were created in the image of God; however, you now bear the scars of sin. God redeems us from our sin through his grace, the sacrifice of His only son, Jesus. Thereby we are transformed, being made into a new creation.

You are no longer in darkness but in the light. You have been washed, blessed with receiving a new self, reborn, and renewed by the Holy Spirit. Use the Spirit to become who God has created you to be, joining Him in the work that He is doing. Know that God is always working, even when He is resting.

He is working because everything is under His control. Nothing happens unless God allows it. He has the blueprint for every life on earth and even on those not yet born.

"Before I formed thee in the belly I knew thee; and before thou camest forth out of the womb I sanctified thee, and I ordained thee a prophet unto the nations." ~ Jeremiah 1:5. [KJV]

I have outlined the components as I best know and understand them. I am not a scholar; however, I am firmly rooted and planted in God's Word. It is up to us to focus on becoming and soaring. We must fulfill God's purpose for our creation. We must focus on becoming and evolving into the person that we need to be in this world.

I have categorized our becoming into stages of life.

Reflection

- Identify your gifts and talents.
- What is your why or calling?
- How are you using your gifts and talents to build up and change this world?

CHAPTER TWO

Stages of Life

As I look back over my life, I see that at each major stage there were milestones. Milestones that added to my character and values. Understand, I see myself forever evolving, growing and learning. We undergo major stages in our life with growth never ceasing to occur until death. Every day you should seek to grow, not ever thinking that you have arrived with nothing left to be learned.

The stages of our life are present for us to glean from. We are to become like a sponge, soaking up wisdom and knowledge bit by bit so that we are equipped to progress forward to the other stages.

Thus far, I am only in stage 3 – Seasoned Adult. I am praying that God will bless me to experience being an elder. My calling is to help and add value to the lives of others. Lifting up those that come behind me to be significant and instrumental in this world is something I love doing as so many did the same for me. I am overjoyed with being able to be His servant, glorifying Him and helping to build up His kingdom.

It's not easy to stand for God. The ruler of this world is winning over the minds of man. He is controlling their thoughts and leading to them being angry, jealous and envious.

The fruit of anger, jealousy and envy is violence and hatred. God is answering mankind now with pandemics, natural disasters and wars. I look back over my life, giving God thanks for the time He has blessed me to live. In the chapters that follow, I will speak on my experiences as a child, an adolescent, a young adult and a seasoned adult.

I will share with you my lessons learned, along with the applications of those lessons to my life. As you read the pages that follow, I ask that you ponder and jot down the lessons that you have learned. Take the time to evaluate and reflect. Without evaluating your life experiences, the lessons are lost and there is no progression.

Adolescent

Adolescence is defined as the period of human growth that occurs between the ages of 10-21. During this time of my life, I was learning about self. I developed a few friendships that would be for life.

As with most adolescents, I spent most of my time with family and friends focusing on playing and having a good time. This is the time when my values were being planted, cultivated and instilled. During this stage of my life, I was a handful.

I recall an incident in grammar school that will forever remain imprinted in my memory. My mother and father impressed into the minds of their children that we were to stand firm. We were to believe in who we were and who was within us.

My mother would always quote Martin Luther King, Jr. to us:

"A man cannot stand on your back unless it is bent."

Martin Luther King, Jr. had a dream. A dream that is instilled in the hearts of many and still lives on today. History will forever be impacted by the vision of this one man. He remained faithful to his cause and purpose, not allowing himself to be distracted or dissuaded. God used him to be an instrument to bring about a change in this world.

Opening the minds and hearts of mankind to all people matters. No one race is better than another. We are all created equal. God made us all with no man having dominion over another man.

I remember having a disagreement with my eighth-grade teacher. All the kids in my class felt she was condescending and disrespectful.

She lacked humility and was very arrogant. Know that because of my parents, I always felt that I had to be the one to speak up. I was always willing to stand up for those who felt oppressed or beat down.

I thought it was my responsibility to be their voice; however, I have since toned down my rush to speak up first and be the loudest. I have learned that others must be willing to take a stand for themselves in order for me to stand for and with them. I do not recall the specifics of our disagreement due to the lapse of time; however, what I do remember most is my behavior and conduct.

Due to my actions, she would not allow me to return to her class. I was scheduled to graduate from eighth grade in two months. Ultimately, common ground was reached with my parents, the teacher and the principal. I was temporarily placed in another eighth-grade class, allowing me to graduate on time.

However, this was the first of a few encounters that would occur in my life that enlightened me regarding the power of one's mind and tongue. When I reflect back on this incident what most sticks with me is that I was disrespectful to my teacher, an elder. I was being disrespectful to a person that God had appointed to be a trainer and instructor.

I have learned that my tongue is a small instrument that can cause one to get into big trouble. It only takes a small match to set a big forest on fire! As I have aged, I see that my tongue is an instrument that I must control, otherwise many of the outcomes in my life would result in much pain and hardship. This little instrument is still one I am constantly working to tame.

"The tongue is also a fire, a world of evil among the parts of the body. It corrupts the whole body, sets the whole course of one's life on fire, and is itself set on fire by hell." ~ James 3:6

I am a witness to the truth in these words. Everything we need to know and learn is written in the Bible. Just open it up and you will find a scripture that you can apply to any situation in your life.

I have allowed my tongue to rule in situations when all I needed to do was be quiet. I have learned that good will always conquer evil. There is no need to say a word or have the last word. God will have the last word. Just be patient and watch.

God had a way of bringing this teacher back into my life. God always has the final say. His Word is true and never fails. Unbeknownst to me I worked out at a local gym where her husband was a member. What is very ironic is that he was part of a group that I would hang out with in the health club. Our group progressed to having lunch on Saturdays or a light snack in the evenings after our workout. We developed relationships that have withstood time.

This was all platonic, thus men and women could be friends without allowing the flesh to rule. Not once did I cross the line with any male in this group.

One night a group of us all went out and guess who showed up, my eighth-grade teacher with the gentlemen from the health club. I was floored.

I thought "Oh boy, this is too much." We both looked at each other with surprise and reflected back on the incident from eighth grade.

We both felt embarrassed and ashamed. We understood we were both at fault and that the incident added to our character. We were on God's potter's wheel. God will use the largest and the smallest incidents in your life to mold you into His vision.

Teaching - Instilling Values

As I progressed during this stage of my life, I received numerous teachings and guidance from my parents. Our household consisted of three children, two girls and one boy. I was blessed to be in a home with both a mother and a father.

My parents drilled into all three of us that we were great, beautiful and exceptional. What parent doesn't want the best for their children?

This is the responsibility of a parent. My mother and father did the best that they could with the resources they had available. My parents were not the greatest; however, their actions portrayed their confidence in themselves, and their deep roots in the Lord. We were not to allow anyone to make us cower. No man was better or greater than any of us.

My mom was from the south, my grandfather was white and my grandmother was black.

Due to their interracial marriage, my mother witnessed firsthand the impacts of the actions resulting from racial inequality. She also had a father that had crossed race lines in the south, marrying a black woman. My mother left the south, moving to Chicago like most blacks who migrated to the north seeking better. My mother traveled to Chicago to grow herself because she believed that the world offered possibilities and opportunities. Due to the other priorities of her generation, education was not on her list of critical needs. Her priority was stability and raising a family.

My mother's goal was to have a husband and a family. Neither my mother and father held a degree past high school; however, this did not make them believe they were inferior.

As I stated before, we were a faith-based household, thus God was the source of our strength. With God, all things are possible. He is the foundation of faith and hope. I have memories of my Mom being vigilant in her reading of the Bible and the Holy Quran. My mother changed religions when I was a toddler.

I was raised as a Muslim but I ultimately changed over to Christianity after college. I have selected Victory Apostolic Church in Matteson, IL as my church home.

As I reflect back in my life, adolescence was a key time for me. It launched my journey to discovery of self. I know that even back then God had me. He was just waiting on me to find and know him. I know that I continue to be on the potter's wheel.

"Yet you, LORD, are our Father. We are the clay; you are the potter; we are all the work of your hand." ~Isaiah 64:8.

God is molding me. I will continue to be molded because I am continuing to evolve, learn and grow. My being molded in His image will never cease until my physical death.

Influencer – One Light Sparking Another

After elementary school, God placed people in my life that were instrumental to my development. I had two women who mentored me, my high school gym teacher Jane Davis, and Georgia Harris, a Vice President in a large pharmaceutical firm.

Prior to my being taken under the wings of my high school gym teacher I aspired to follow in the footsteps of my brother and sister by developing a trade. College was not on my radar or a possibility. As I said previously, my parents did not have a formal education, thus my environment would have limited my potential. Because my parents had not been exposed to formal education, college was not discussed or even explored in my household.

It was because of Ms. Davis that I went to college. She saw the potential and possibilities that were within me. I will forever be indebted to her for befriending me and being one of many mentors in my life.

Without her, I would have wasted the gifts and talents in which God had planted within me. She saw that which was within me that I was oblivious to see. Ms. Davis saw what I could be instead of focusing on what I was.

My mother and father lived a good life. There was nothing wrong with obtaining a skilled trade and not pursuing continuing education past high school. My father had served in the military and worked for about 40 years for the railroad.

They were good role models living an average life, they were not in pursuit of being exceptional. They were complacent and enjoyed life as it was. I thank Ms. Davis greatly for the fire in her that led to sparking the light that was within me. She has since passed away; however, she will forever be a person who was influential in my life.

Let me move on to the second instrumental person in my life during this stage, Georgia Harris. Ms. Harris was a business executive, and the Vice President of a large pharmaceutical company. She was a leader that others willingly followed.

She was a woman of influence, well respected, a communicator and a person that valued others. She is the person that today I seek to still emulate and follow.

She understood that leadership is not based on a title. True leadership is about reaching back to help others, learning what is in the heart of others, and how you can help others get what they want.

She allowed me to work at the corporation in the summer months while I was in college. This allowed me to earn money while also learning from her.

It is because of Ms. Harris and Ms. Davis that I understood that I must give back. I must reach back to help those that are behind me and walk with me, otherwise I am failing God by not being a Contributor and Giver, but instead being a Taker. I seek to be a river not a reservoir.

Foundation - Withstand

I stress that during this time in your life, developing and forging relationships with people of influence is key. It is vital that we surround ourselves with people of good character. Learning from others who can add value to you and which you can emulate will help mold and grow you into the person God intends for you to be.

1 Corinthians 15:33 counsels us, "Do not be misled: Bad company corrupts good character."

I know many times our focus is on hanging out with the crowd and being popular; however, hanging with the popular crowd, rather than the God inspired crowd, provides no gain or benefit. Recall the story in the Bible when the people were rioting against the Apostle Paul because he was teaching that man should not be a worshipper of idols, but of God.

The people were rioting, and like many crowds today, most of the people did not even know what they were rioting about. They were just following the crowd. Following the crowd will not get you to where you need to go or closer to what you can become. God does want each of us to enjoy our life but we also must maintain our focus on Him.

This is the time for you to develop self-discipline and perseverance. The character traits that I developed during this period in my life laid the foundation for who I have evolved into today.

They have become the building blocks that have added tremendously to the journey of my life. I have gotten off track at times, but my foundation has remained secure.

I may have learned some hard lessons, but I did not topple or become uprooted. I am continuing to add strength and depth to my roots. They are deeply rooted from a lifetime of challenges, and allow me to withstand. When I reflect on my foundation it brings to mind the book of Daniel. There are three illustrations of those who did not break with pressure, but withstood.

One, Daniel was selected to serve in the king's palace; however, he remained faithful and obedient to God and his commands.

He did not allow man to influence his beliefs or practices. Daniel was in the world, but chose not to be of the world, or turn his back on God. From the beginning when he was taken into the king's court, he refused to defile himself by eating the king's food and wine.

Daniel wasn't arrogant or demanding with his refusal to eat from the King's table. He worked "within the system," politely convincing the king's cook to let him and his friends eat their own diet.

He showed the king how not following the crowd made him better. His eating fruits, vegetables and water led to him looking better, and the king changing his attitude. The king continued to change his way of thinking about Daniel, ultimately placing Daniel in a high position in his court.

When you follow God, as Daniel did, it will cause man to see the brightness of your light, the power within you and the God who is sustaining you. Two, three other obedient followers, Shadrach, Meshach, and Abednego refused to bow and worship an idol which would have been in violation of God's commandments.

"You shall have no other gods before me." ~ Deuteronomy 5:7.

In this incident the king had issued a decree that all in his kingdom were to fall down and worship an image of gold. Failure to worship the image would result in being thrown into a blazing furnace.

Their disobedience to a man in order to be obedient to God meant they were sentenced to be thrown into a blazing furnace. The king thought the men were going to beg him for mercy; however, they showed the king who was in control. Shadrach, Meshach, and Abednego informed the king that they did not need to defend themselves. They told the king that the God they served was able to deliver them from the furnace and the king's hand.

Furthermore they stated, "But even if he does not, we want you to know, your Majesty, that we will not serve your gods or worship the image of gold you have set up." ~ Daniel 3:18.

The three men refused to turn from God, resolving to not break but to withstand.

Isaiah 7:9 states, "If you do not stand in your faith,
you will not stand at all."

The men were all thrown into a furnace so hot that the soldiers throwing them into the flames died. But, not one hair was burned or singed on any of the three men. God delivered and protected. His power is beyond man and incomprehensible.

Idols are useless and have no power. They cannot rescue anyone in distress nor provide or sustain anyone in times of trials. When we think of idols, we may think of statues and laugh at the thought that anyone could believe a wooden or metal idol had power. But there are other idols we do worship and do believe have power to change our lives.

Many who are of the world worship money, gold and other tangible assets; however, not one of these things can move a mountain or can be called upon when in dire need.

I have not witnessed one person call on money to save them from disease, cancer or a bullet but I have witnessed them call on the name of Jesus who saves and heals.

Three, in Daniel 3, King Darius passed a decree that no one was to pray to any god for the next 30 days. Disobedience would result in being thrown into a den of lions. but Daniel didn't waiver. He obeyed God because he knew what God had said:

"You shall not bow down to them or worship them; for I, the LORD
your God, am a jealous God." ~ Deuteronomy 5:9.

I have read many stories in the Old Testament about God getting angry with the outcome of death and punishment. I for one am like Daniel. I hear God loud and clear. I am not worshipping anyone but the LORD. Daniel stayed devoted to the Lord and continued to pray. He continued his devotion of praying three times a day.

No decree was going to stop him from worshiping the Lord. Daniel was remaining faithful to God. He chose to stand and not break. Daniel's failure to follow the decree resulted in him being put into a den of lions to be eaten alive, or torn limb from limb. But not a lion touched him.

Daniel survived because God sent his angel who shut the mouths of the lions. Daniel's loyalty and obedience to God resulted in him being protected from his enemies and the evil intent they held towards him.

He had not done any wrong to God, in fact he glorified the Lord, remaining faithful in worshipping only Him. I have applied this same principle to my life. Do not break – withstand.

"The Lord is my rock, my fortress, and my deliverer, my God is my rock, in whom I take refuge, my shield and the horn of my salvation and stronghold." — Psalms 18:103.

If you are doing what is right, following God and His commandments and laws, no man or woman will be able to harm you. No matter the consequences, you must remain faithful to God and his commandments. You must not break but withstand. Know that God is greater than any problem, man or woman can throw at you. Do not bow down, cower or allow anyone to influence who you are, and to whom you belong.

"For I have kept the ways of the Lord, I am not guilty of turning from my God." ~ Psalm 18:21.

I stress, do not turn from God. He is the one that can and will provide. He will sustain and deliver you from evil and protect you from those seeking to do you harm. He will keep you safe in the fiery furnace and close the mouths of lions.

Do not break – WITHSTAND. Build your house on a solid foundation that will withstand a storm.

"Therefore, everyone who hears these words of mine and puts them into practice is like a wise man who built his house on the rock. The rain came down, streams rose, and the winds blew and broke against that house; yet it did not fall, because it had a foundation on the rock." ~ Matthew 7:24

If anyone seeks to dissuade or persuade me from the Lord, he/she cannot be in my circle, nor will I be listening to anything they have to say. I will remove myself from their presence. I wish them the best in their life. As for my house, we will follow the LORD and His commands at all times.

Reflection

- What are the lessons that shaped you when you were adolescent?
- How have you applied the lessons to your life?
- How are you making growth a continual process and commitment?
- What is your plan for making growth a continual commitment?
- What are the top 3 values that are the foundation of your life? How are you applying and incorporating these values into your life?
- During your period of adolescence, who were the top two mentors in your life? What impact did they have on your life? How has this impact shaped your purpose?

CHAPTER THREE

Young Adult | Molding and Building Character

Our life is a race where we are seeking a prize and getting to the finish line. In a race only one person gets the prize; however, in the race of our life we are all winners.

As part of our race, you need to determine what is the purpose for which you are running.

The Apostle Paul says it best, "run in such a way as to get the prize."
~ 1 Corinthians 9:24.

We are running a race for an everlasting crown.. For your race, you must identify what is your cause and why you embrace it. It is good to have fun and enjoy life; however, you must set goals and clarify the purpose of your existence.

Each of us will be called to duty, it is our responsibility to answer and accept the call. God created you and I for a purpose.

Our purpose is not to cruise through life and not give back. You were created because God has work for you to do to glorify Him and to add value to His kingdom.

"For he chose us in Him before the creation of the world to be holy and blameless in His sight. In love He predestined us for adoption to sonship through Jesus Christ, in accordance with His pleasure and will."
~ Ephesians 1:4-5.

We must release the yoke of slavery to sin and embrace being a slave to righteousness. We are blessed to be slaves of God. The Apostle Paul stated that when he was called, he did not consult with men or ask others what they were doing and why. He did not go see who was doing what work and why.

Paul was on his way to Damascus to continue his persecution of God's disciples when God called him to duty. God temporarily blinded him. Upon receiving back his sight, he washed and ate to refresh, replenish and prepare.

Paul took up his mantle to perform the work God had for him to do. As with Paul, when God calls, we are to answer.

"Know that your labor in the Lord is not in vain."
~ 1 Corinthians 15:58.

Serving the Lord is a privilege. God is always at work. It is a privilege to be invited to join him. It is a blessing to be an instrument for God.

Our efforts in service will be greatly rewarded with everlasting blessings that are incomprehensible. As such, we cannot allow ourselves to become distracted and distressed by the things of the world.

Keep focused on your duty being of the world but in this world being a light and beacon. You are an instrument for the Lord.

Relationship with God

I stress developing a relationship with the Lord. You need to accept him as your Lord and Savior, putting Him first above all else. First seek His kingdom and the rest will follow. Placing God first will equip you to handle that which is in store for you later. Know that your life will have adversity. There will be storms, trials and hardship. This is life.

If you had no adversity in life, then you would not grow and progress. Know and believe that you will soar above adversity finding better ground. A strong and solid foundation with the Lord will help you handle that which is to come.

Seeking God will aid in your finding and uncovering who you are. Do not wander aimlessly through life wasting time that is precious and should be used wisely.

There will be time later to enjoy the fruits of your labor. John Maxwell says it best "pay now and play later."

Now is the time to pay. Identify your key values, determine your key values, formulate the pillars of your life and set goals for your life.

As you set your goals, you must work on establishing and developing relationships with those who can sharpen and add value to you. If you are the smartest person in your group, how will you grow? How will you develop? How will you see what is possible? Where there are opportunities? Let your circle be composed of people who are evolving, have aspirations and whom you can be of service.

Your Circle

Let's look at your circle. Your circle should be composed of people who are like-minded and who add value to you while you add value to them. Everyone within your circle should share the common traits of growing, learning and evolving.

Not everyone will be at the same level of growth. Some will have more to offer than you, and others will have less. It's not that you're on the exact same place on the path, but that you're on the same path.

At times some of you will rush ahead, and some will fall behind as they encounter challenges, but you all walk with and in sight of each other. You will experience times when you lend a hand to others, and times when they extend a hand to help you. Remember that.

King Solomon stated, "Walk with the wise and become wise, for a companion of fools suffers harm." ~ Proverbs 13:20.

Your circle will change and evolve as you progress through life. The people which I had as key companions in the earlier stages of my life are not the same people that are within my circle today. I love and have learned from them all. It's like looking at a library of people, not books.

I can say, "I remember her, or him and what I learned," just as we can look at books on our bookshelves. We may not be reading or interacting with everyone we've read or met, but they're still a part of us.

It doesn't hurt to think about what we've learned from past mentors and friends. We can still learn from their wisdom.

There's an old saying I love every time I hear it or share it:

"People come into your life for a reason, a season or a lifetime. When you know which one it is, you will know what to do for that person."

When someone is in your life for a **REASON,** it is usually to meet a need you have expressed, or that God wants you to meet. They may be there to help you navigate a challenge, a loss, some difficulty or situation.

They are a godsend, meant to provide you with guidance and support, to aid you physically, emotionally, or spiritually. Once that reason has been resolved, without any rhyme or reason the relationship will end. They may be offended, or die, or move, or simply find someone else to help.

But they've helped you and then moved on. The prayer of yours has been answered and it's time for them to go.

Some people come into your life for a **SEASON,** because your turn has come to share, grow or learn. Like summer, fall, or spring or winter, they come for a short time, bringing light, peace, friendship, and laughter.

They may teach you something, or merely provide friendship for a brief time, then they too are gone. God intended them only for a season. They will be like leaves on a tree. Just as old leaves are discarded and die at the end of the season to make room for new leaves (people) to sprout and bloom for your next season.

People throughout your life will come and go. As you surround yourself with others who have similar beliefs and values you'll see your life and your friendships change.

You will attract people who reflect who you are, and who you are becoming. Let your focus be on evolving and growing, not on holding onto relationships that feel comfortable. We all love old, broken in shoes because they're familiar and comfortable.

That doesn't mean they're good for our feet — just that they are comfortable. But what joy we feel when we get a new pair of shoes. I'm not saying no one will ever be around for long.

Some people are in your life for life, and nothing will cause them to leave. God has them there for *His* reasons. The closer you are to God, and your inner circle, the more quickly you'll recognize who is there for a reason, a season, or for life.

Life is not just about making a living and partying on the weekend.

God intended your life to be significant and impactful. The people in your circle should be like-minded, consistently blowing up their box reaching new plateaus. As you go along, you will notice an ebb and flow of friends. You'll gain new friends, and lose some. Don't be saddened by this. You have to leave behind that which is holding you back.

You must discard old ways of thinking and habits, and the people who keep you bound to those old habits. Life is a continuous journey.

Your destination will not be reached until you die. Your ultimate destination is death. Until death, you are to live a fulfilling life in your purpose. Each day seek to add value to your life and to those around you.

Examples of your circle are illustrated both by Jesus and the Apostle Paul. Jesus surrounded himself with twelve disciples, all of whom he picked. His inner circle consisted of John, James and Peter. There was Christ's circle of twelve, and his inner circle of three.

Each disciple sharpened one another. They each held one another up so they could perform the work that had been predestined for them. After Jesus left to return to the Father, He tasked his circle with continuing to spread the gospel and establish His church. Apostle Paul's circle was Barnabas, Titus, Luke, Timothy, John Mark and Silas.

All worked together in spreading the gospel and bringing people to Christ. Just as Christ and Paul selected their inner circle of men willing to grow and learn, your circle should be composed of those who are seeking to evolve and grow. You must stretch to reach new plateaus and boundaries. Your continual journey in growth will require the help of others.

Proverbs 27:17 says it best, "As iron sharpens irons, so one person sharpens another."

Your circle will include those who are doing the work that you are seeking to do so that you can continue in your growth and learning. You were created to soar. You must continually be pursuing higher ground and new plateaus. The people in your circle will provide you with support, motivation, inspiration, and resilience.

Ecclesiastes 4:10 states *"Pity anyone who falls and has no one to help them up."*

The people in your circle are to lift you up and not knock you down. John Maxwell stated:

"The most significant factor in any person's environment is the people. If you change nothing else in your life for the better than that, you will have increased your chances of success tenfold."

I must repeat myself, if you are the smartest person in your circle then you are not growing. You will have no one to emulate or use as a role model. God may call you to be the strongest or smartest in the group so you can mentor others for a season. But He expects us to surround ourselves with others who qualities are the ones that you are seeking to develop and others who are seeking to grow.
Sue Enquist stated:

"Live in the 33% rule. Hang with the top third of people, they are dream makers. Middle third: blow in the wind.
Bottom third: suck the life out of you."

Surround yourself with people who are dreamers that take action and support you in sharpening your skills, and those who will support you in your pursuit of building a better life. Be consistent and persistent in going further in life where you are continually progressing and striving forward. If you do this you will notice people will come and go as they grow as well as surrounding themselves with people who can strengthen them as well. Don't take it personally. It's the natural cycle of growth. One day you will need to move on, other times those you look up to will move on.

Focus on Living Each Day

Focusing on living each day of your life. Don't ruminate or wallow in the failures and shortcomings of the day before, and don't look or worry about what tomorrow will bring.

Set priorities and goals daily and weekly, but focus on the day before you. Be continually planning and executing. You must be consistent, insistent, and persistent.

Do not rush through your life. Embrace and seize each day. If you rush, you will miss the valuable lessons that may possibly make a road dead end where you should have made a turn.

Evaluated experience is the best and hardest teacher. Tests are given with the lesson being learned afterwards only if you take the time to pause and reflect. You must embrace the experiences with application of what you have learned.

You must live each day to its fullest. Focus on today. Jesus said when you pray say:

"Give us today our daily bread." ~ *Matthew 6:11.*

This means God meets our needs each day so each day is important. Find a way to value each day leading to investing in today.

Les Brown stated,
"The world is waiting for you to wake up to the person you are called to be.

"Stop listening to the negative inner conversation that's causing you to play small. Focus your mind on positive thoughts, possibilities and solutions that can move you forward. Tap into your creativity and determination and stay busy. Stay focused."

Many times I have heard "I can't wait until Friday, and the week-end." I would often hear this on Monday. I would think, what about the other five days of the week?

This type of thinking is due to being unfocused and unfulfilled. Working a job or a career that is not bringing you joy, happiness and fulfillment contributes to this mindset.

This kind of life approach is just coasting along—drifting on a boat with no course. This is a negative attitude. You are allowing negative thinking to control your life and allowing obstacles to be placed in your mind. In essence, you are not treasuring the gift of life and making the most of each day.

Proverbs 27:1 says, "Do not boast about tomorrow, for you do not know what a day may bring."

You should not be focusing only on living for two days a week. Make each day count. Each day is worthy of itself.

James says it best, "Why, you do not even know what will happen tomorrow. What is your life? You are a mist that appears for a little while and then vanishes." ~ James 4:14.

For tomorrow you may not be blessed to wake up but today you have been gifted with life. Let each day stand on its own. Give each day your best and be focused. Not focusing on today may result in your missing out on opportunities.

Each day God has blessings in store for you. He has plans for your life. God has work for you to perform in His kingdom. Embrace each day as a new day of learning. Strive to progress forward in the fulfillment of the goals that you have for your life.

Focus each day on deepening and strengthening your relationship with the Lord. Ask Him to speak to you so that you know the way to travel. Living your life is like a gift that should be unwrapped daily. Maximize the time in each day.

Progress forward in realizing your dreams and becoming who God has predestined you to be.

Les Brown states, "in every day, there are 1,440 minutes. That means we have 1,440 daily opportunities to make a positive impact."

Set goals daily — prioritizing, reevaluating, strategizing and energizing your life. Embrace each day believing that it is filled with opportunities that will promote your learning and growing. You are getting closer to BECOMING. If the job you are working is not your calling, then I challenge you to develop a plan to get to your calling instead of focusing on rushing through your life.

Develop a growth plan and implement the plan, setting measurable milestones and tasks. Live for Today. Embrace today with vigor and purpose.

Don't Settle

We tend to rush through life because we have settled. We have become comfortable and programmed with where we are. We don't want to change. We want to keep on going along in our familiar, comfortable way. We think that the way we're traveling now is the only way.

This results in our accepting being average and not striving to be exceptional. We may be working a job where we are discontent. We are just making it through and dreading going into the office each day.

But we accept it. We've settled for what it is. We have settled with a spouse or significant other because we just wanted some shoes under our bed or a warm body next to us. We have to stop settling. Know that better is always an option. Better is what each of us should inspire to reach. Prior to embracing my purpose and cause, I was one of those people that dreaded Monday. When Sunday arrived, my whole day was in mourning.

I felt like on Monday that I was going to the guillotine. I was unhappy in my job. I allowed my job to be the focal point of my life. Yes, employment is vital to our living in this world; however, we cannot allow a job to drain our mind, spirit and soul.

At the time, I did not understand that there was more than one answer. Working a job to please others is not the only answer. Some of us are born with an entrepreneurial spirit, we are free. I saw things as black and white, as either, or. I saw my job, whether I liked it or not, as the only answer in my life. I had it or I didn't have anything. This is a fallacy that many of us fall into. It is a trap that we have allowed to take root becoming cemented into our way of thinking.

Our mind is power. What we focus on is what we expand upon. I was so focused on being unhappy and the issues at work instead of the possibilities and opportunities for my life. I had tunnel vision. I woke up to being programmed, which led to my reprogramming my mind. I broke through the barrier I had placed in my mind. I changed my mindset. This is what each of us must do in order to overcome the obstacles in our life.

If we don't take charge of our mindset, we will live a life of discontent, depression, and discouragement. We will miss out on the beauty of life and how wonderful it can be. We will miss out on what can be when focusing on that which is and can be changed. We will fail the One who has gifted us with life and our talents.

You must identify the prize you are seeking. Who are you? What is your cause? What is your purpose? Understand you may not have the full picture of what is possible. Clarity will come with time; however, you must develop a basic understanding of where you want to go.

Take an inventory of your skills, strengths, and weaknesses. What brings you enjoyment and fuels your mind? You must train your body and mind. You are running a race that you can win.

Be positive in your thinking, thoughts, and action. The prize you seek may be wealth; however, know that wealth fades and can be taken away. There is one place where your wealth and treasures can't be stolen:

"Lay not up for yourselves treasures upon earth, where moth and rust doth corrupt, and where thieves break through and steal: But lay up for yourselves treasures in heaven, where neither moth nor rust doth corrupt, and where thieves do not break through nor steal:

For where your treasure is, there will your heart be also."
~Matthew 6:19-21.

Define what success means to you. To me, success is adding value to others who in turn will add value to this world. Thus, we both become significant and impactful. I call this the power of adding value.

Wealth will come because God will bless you with the resources to continue doing the work for which you have been created. Remember, God blesses us with riches so that we in turn we will share and redistribute, utilizing what we have been gifted in his kingdom to help his children.

Wealth is good for you to be comfortable and equip you with resources. However, I stress that you keep your focus on the prize that is beyond this world. Run your race keeping your focus on the Lord.

The rewards you receive from Him cannot compare to what is to come. Ultimately you are seeking to hear "well done" being blessed with a transformed body and a new world.

You will be a new creation, shedding the body and things of this world. Recall the rich young man in Mark 10:17-27.

The young man came up to Jesus and asked Him what must he do to be saved. Jesus said, As Jesus started on his way, a man ran up to him and fell on his knees before him. "Good teacher," he asked, "what must I do to inherit eternal life?"

"Why do you call me good?" Jesus answered. "No one is good—except God alone. You know the commandments: 'You shall not murder, you shall not commit adultery, you shall not steal, you shall not give false testimony, you shall not defraud, honor your father and mother.'"
"Teacher," he declared, "all these I have kept since I was a boy."

Jesus looked at him and loved him. "One thing you lack," he said. "Go, sell everything you have and give to the poor, and you will have treasure in heaven. Then come, follow me." At this reply the man's face fell with great disappointment.

He went away sad, because he had great wealth. The rich man was devastated. He idolized his wealth more than he loved God. He was not willing to sacrifice or give up his wealth for the Lord. Notice, Jesus didn't ever tell anyone else to "sell everything and follow me." He only told this young man to do so.

He just told his other disciples to, "follow me." He saw however that this young man kept the other commandments and laws, just as he insisted he did.

But Jesus also saw into the young man's heart and saw the idol he worshipped — money. Remember, it's not money that's evil. It's the *love* of money that causes problems.

"For the love of money is the root of all evil: which while some coveted after, they have erred from the faith, and pierced themselves through with many sorrows." ~ 1 Timothy 6:10.

Run Your Race

In 1 Corinthians 9, the Apostle Paul provides an analogy of runners in a race, comparing it to the spiritual race that Christians run. Physical runners must become conditioned, training their body for endurance, stamina and strength.

Each is seeking to be the winner, but there is only one winner who claims the crown. The race is a competition because only one can be the winner. However, for us as Christians, we are all winners.

However, just like runners, we must train and prepare, preparing our mind and body for endurance, perseverance, and strength. We must be resilient.

In our race we are fighting not only against those in the world, but the one who is ruling this world. You must put on the full armor of God. You must strengthen yourself for battle to run the Christian race.

"Put on the full armor of God, so that you can take your stand against the devil's schemes."— Ephesians 6:11

Keep your focus on obtaining a crown that is everlasting. Concentrate on the race where you will reach the finish line, without being disqualified because you choose to conform and follow the world instead. You have a purpose and a call to duty that must be fulfilled.

Paul says it best:
"Therefore, I do not run like someone running aimlessly; I do not fight like a boxer beating the air. No, I strike a blow to my body and make it my slave so that I have preached to others, I myself will not be disqualified for the prize." — 1 Corinthians 9:26-27.

Use your body, mind and spirit to win the ultimate prize. Be a slave in the service of the Lord not of this world. Know that what God offers is for everyone. All are welcome to run in the race. You must be willing to deny self, instead living for God and the Spirit.

Reflection
- What is the purpose for the race you are running? What prize are you seeking?
- How would you describe your relationship with the Lord?
- How are you maximizing your time each day or each week? There are 168 hours in every week, how are you using your time?
- What are you consistently doing each day to progress? There are five things that I do each day — read, write, reflect, connect and organize.
- Who do you have in your inner circle? How are you keeping one another focused?

CHAPTER FOUR

The Seasoned Adult

I am on the journey of fulfilling my purpose. I am casting my vision and constantly evolving. I continually reach goals and set new goals. I am striving to become the person for which I was created. I have had failures; however, I do not call them failures because I call them lessons.

Lessons that I have become guides in my life. They have unveiled opportunities and possibilities because I have a Godly vision for my life. There's nothing wrong with having a vision for your life.

Joseph was a strategic planner, casting a vision at God's direction to store up food in preparation for a seven year drought.

"And the Lord answered me, and said, Write the vision, and make it plain upon tables, that he may run that readeth it."
~ Habakkuk 2:2. [KJV]

Along with my lessons, I have had victories, big and small to which I rejoice along the way. I rejoice at all times. 1 Thessalonians 5:16-18 says:

"Rejoice always, pray continually, give thanks in all circumstances, for this is God's will for you in Christ Jesus."

I am proud of the person to which I am evolving into and becoming. The progress that I am making each day of my life. It does not matter what others think or believe because the one who matters is God. I know that I am making progress when I have reached a milestone thus, I celebrate! Join me in daily rejoicing and being thankful.

Progression

Do not take for granted the small victories or progression. Progress is worth celebrating. It illuminates your dedication and accomplishments. Progress is making strides or steps towards your purpose. You must remain consistent which requires time, effort, sweat and heartache.

You must remain dedicated and persistent. Enjoy and rejoice in each step in your journey. You are continuously growing and improving because growth never stops. Growth is a requirement for us to evolve and progress.

Benjamin Franklin states "Without continual growth and progress, such words as improvement, achievement, and success have no meaning."

As you journey through your life, you will continue to gain resilience and build your character.

Olympian track and field star Carl Lewis stated "It is all about the journey not the outcome."

Your journey, including the downs and struggles as well as the victories, is where you develop a greater understanding of the Lord. You develop deep roots in faith and hope during hard times as you lean more on the Lord.

You understand that with God all things are possible even when they appear impossible. This is how you develop your faith — by trusting God in good times and bad.

He will provide as long as you are doing the work that he has planned for your life. You must remain faithful to Him and His Word. Keep your hope in Him. Hope is essential. Believe in that which can be and the outcome will come as you have expected.

Recall the Israelites, God freed them from slavery and gifted them with the Promised Land— a land overflowing with milk and honey. A land that would provide for all their needs and fulfill their desires. All was being provided to them.

The hard work and labor had been done by those who currently occupied the land. The Israelites only had to undergo a journey to get to the Promised Land.

They made progress every step of the way but instead of celebrating, they complained. They complained that there was no water and food; however, God continuously provided food and water—providing manna and quail. Not once did they hunger for food or water.

Just as amazing was the fact their clothing and shoes never wore out. Imagine clothing that withstands 40 years. Fashion stood still. Instead of rejoicing in their progress. They choose to complain at each turn and every step in the journey. The Israelites continually doubted God and His power.

Due to their lack of faith, God had them wander aimlessly in the desert for 40 years when they could have reached the promised land in 10 days. At each progression in your life, you are to enjoy the journey.

Do not become like the Israelites complaining about the journey. You are to enjoy and celebrate. Rejoice in your progress as milestones are achieved.

God is watching and overseeing your progression. You are participating in the journey that has been predestined for your life. He will not let you fail. God will provide what you need. Enjoy, celebrate and rejoice!

God is watching you to see how you will handle the journey. Upon reaching a goal, the journey does not end. Goal setting is an ongoing, continuous process in life. You must continually strive for progress and improvement.

As you reach one goal or milestone, there is another, and another. God has much work for you to do in his kingdom, thus your work will never be done.

"The harvest is plentiful but the workers are few. Ask the Lord of the harvest, therefore, to send out workers into his harvest field."
~ Matthew 9:37-38.

In your life, you will continue to climb to new heights. You will continue to make progress because you are consistent and persistent. The journey illustrates your growth, progress and improvement. You are being prepared to fulfill your purpose.

"Every day you may make progress. Every step may be fruitful. Yet there will stretch out before you an ever-lengthening, ever-ascending, ever-improving path. You know you will never get to the end of the journey…
But this, so far from discouraging, only adds
to the joy and glory of the climb." ~ Winston Churchill

Not Average

The next time you are looking at yourself in the mirror, recite these words out loud:. "You are not average! You are outstanding! You are dynamic. You are God's creation and created in His image. You have His greatness dwelling within you and His Spirit."

You must be willing to stretch yourself beyond what you know and have falsely determined that you are incapable of achieving. Do not settle for being average or developing a mindset to be average.

Edmund Gaudet stated **"*Being "average" is to take up space for no purpose; to take the trip through life, but never to pay the fare; to return no interest for God's investment in you.*"**

Being average means that you do not have faith in the Lord, and you are not trusting in His will for your life. You are failing to believe in the gifts HE has planted within you.

"In Him we were also chosen, having been predestined according to the plan of him who works out everyone in conformity of his will."
~Ephesians 1:11.

"God's gift to us is potential. Our gift to God: is developing it."
~Author Unknown.

In return for God's investment in you, you are required to believe in yourself. You must go beyond the boundaries that you see resulting in stretching. Being willing to stretch yourself beyond the limits leads to becoming uncomfortable, which in turn leads to growth.

Law 10 of the 15 Invaluable Laws of Growth by John C. Maxwell states *"Life begins at the end of our comfort zone. We go there by stretching."*

Just when you think you cannot go beyond your boundaries, you must stretch further. Believe in God's Word and promises for your life as well as yourself. You are capable and can do it.

You must be willing to make a decision to step out on your faith to receive what God has planned and predestined for your life. You must make a decision to act. Stretch yourself and reach new dimensions.

Make the decisions that lead to growing, learning and transforming. Some will be hard, others will be easy. Develop the discipline to approach both, knowing God has a plan for each.

"Faith by itself, if it is not accompanied by action, is dead."
~ James 2:17.

Be like the rubber band. Its full potential is realized only when it is used. It must be stretched to reach its full potential and in order to fulfill the purpose for which it was created.

Be willing to stretch yourself to go beyond average. Give God back a return in His investment in you.

"Never underestimate the power of dreams and the influence of the human spirit. We are all the same in this notion: The potential for greatness lives within each of us." ~ Wilma Rudolph

Do Not Doubt

As you get closer to God and begin honing in on fulfilling your purpose, the attacks in your mind from the devil will get more intense. By this one simple act you have caught the devil's attention. But he's not the only one.

> *"The thief comes only to steal and kill and destroy. but I have come that they may have life, and have it to the full."* ~ *John 10:10*

Who is the thief? It can be the devil, or it can be friends who are tired of you always being immersed in church or God's Word.

Thieves come in all shapes, sizes and temptations. Do you think Eve would have tasted the apple if she hadn't been curious and tempted? The devil's temptations can look a lot like a blessing!

The devil seeks to have you doubt the Lord, and he uses people and things you don't suspect to help him do just that. The devil does not want you to believe in God's Word and promises.

Further, friends or family that you had in your circle may not continue to be in your circle the more you follow Jesus. You may need to change direction and replenish your circle. Be mindful of who you associate with, they may cause you to doubt the Lord and turn away from Him.

In 2 Kings 6, there was a great famine in Samaria due to the Israelite's disobedience to the Lord. The king of Israel sought to blame the prophet Elisha. As such, he sought to kill him.

The king understood that the current famine was due to the Lord and thus asked why he should continue to wait on the Lord. Elisha responded that the Lord was going to supply food the next day, ending the famine. The officer who was with the king did not believe Elisha and said as much. The officer did not believe the Lord would provide. He foolishly stated:

> *"Look even if the LORD should open the floodgates of heavens, could this happen?"* ~ *2 Kings 7:2.*

The officer either had no faith or he did not believe in the power of the Lord. He was a bad influence on the king. The king allowed both his hardship and this officer within his circle to influence his faith in the Lord.

"I urge you, brothers and sisters, to watch out for those who cause divisions and put obstacles in your way that are contrary to the teaching you have learned. Keep away from them." ~ Romans 16:17.

The king did not have faith that was able to withstand the test or challenge. He did not believe that the Lord would provide. He turned his back on God's Word and promises. The officer within the king's circle did not sharpen him as iron sharpen irons. Instead, he dulled the faith of the king.

However, the Lord was working behind the scenes. The Lord caused the Arameans that were laying siege to Samaria to abandon their camp. They left behind an abundance of food, clothing, gold and silver. The provisions of the Arameans camp ended the famine in Samaria. It took another officer in the circle of the king to make him believe. Those within your circle should help in the building of your faith and support your relationship with the Lord.

Do not allow the devil to get a foothold in your mind. Focus on God's Word instead of the negative words that are being implanted by the devil. He is trying to poison your mind leading to your doubting the Lord.

Kick him out of your mind. Lean on God the same way we trust in the chairs we sit in. We trust a chair to hold our weight. Let us trust God to carry us through whatever challenges or dark times we're facing. Let your thoughts rest on Him and not on the devil.

The devil doesn't hang out with those who are living in sin. They're already in his camp. He wants people who are following God and are in God's camp. He is seeking to attack us *more* because God is moving in our lives.

Have you ever been on a diet and started losing weight? What happens? People notice. Some will cheer you on and encourage you.

But some will suddenly start offering you cakes and sweets, or inviting you to a Sunday dinner where there is temptation to stray from your diet.

It may be unintentional, or unconscious, but some people just don't like to see you winning your battles. The devil is the same way. Let us stand firm with the Lord and on His Words not the devil.

Reflection

How are you stretching, and moving from average to exceptional?

How are you recording and celebrating your progress and victories?

What do you do to remain positive during times of uncertainty and adversity?

What ways do you doubt yourself? How can you remain positive when doubt attempts to take over your mind?

CHAPTER FIVE

The Elder

I haven't yet reached this stage, but I look forward to it. I am still in the pruning and seasoning stage as an adult. When I do reach this stage in my life, I believe it will cause me to reflect upon the legacy that I seek to leave behind.

When I think of *"my legacy,"* I'm not being materialistic. A legacy is something of importance you leave behind for others. Some leave money, some leave property or things.

My legacy is, I pray, a spiritual and emotional legacy. I want to leave behind the kind of life and faith where others will see the Lord but not me. They will see how the Lord worked within and through me.

I do, and I will question myself when I become an elder. I will ask myself, "Did I live a life that was significant and impactful? Did I add value to others and build up others?"

I seek to leave an imprint upon the world. I strive to make a difference in the lives of those that I touch and that are within my reach.

I seek to be remembered as a person that valued, and added value, to the lives of others — a person who strived to lift up others and not tear them down. I envision that during this stage of my life I will be a river that is flowing out to feed many waterfalls. I pray the legacy I leave will be one where I mentored and inspired others to take up their mantle. I enjoy helping others find their purpose and calling. I look to my mentor, John Maxwell, who is in his 70s and still going strong.

He has no plans to retire because he enjoys what he does and believes in what he is doing. This same principle applies to me. I have worked in corporate America and the government for about 35 years of my life.

I am dedicated to giving back, thus I am dedicated to serving and helping others.

I have many stories to share and I know there will be many more opportunities to come where I can help guide others to their path and along their journey.

I look to the elders in my life now and I learn from others who have gone before me. There is a member in my church named Mother Jordan who is 90 + years old and counting.

She is a blessing to me and untold numbers of others. She is still pursuing that which drives her. She is a dedicated servant and actively seeks to help others. I seek to emulate her once I reach this stage in my life. I say to all of you, stay tuned. I am not done yet and I have a way to go.

My ultimate goal when I come to my earthly end is to be able to say:

"I have fought the good fight, I have finished the race,
I have kept the faith." ~2 Timothy 4:7.

Lessons Learned

During the 50 years of my life, I have learned many invaluable lessons. I learned that no one person can be an island. If my dream only includes me then my dream is too small.

One is too small a number to make a significant impact or difference. In the earlier stages of my life, I was a loner and did not understand the value of a circle.

Remember, even Christ had 12 disciples and He was full God and fully man! I had the misconception that I did not need others to collaborate and sharpen me.

As I have progressed through life, I understand that I cannot do anything without God. After God, I need to have a circle and establish connections with others in order to make a difference and be impactful. If I am the only person on my team then my dream is too small.

In the chapters that follow I will outline the key lessons to which I have learned and the application to my life.

Reflection:

- What is your vision, purpose or cause?
- What is the impact you are seeking to make?
- Who is in your community?
- How are you involving others in your community in your dream?

CHAPTER SIX

Mentoring

L et's look at the story of Moses and Joshua in the Bible. Moses mentored Joshua, who became his successor in leading the Israelites. Moses mentored Joshua because Moses had angered God. God had determined that Moses, due to his disobedience to God, would not enter the Promised Land. So Moses had to equip Joshua to carry on for him. In our lives we will meet mentors that will do the same for each of us.

They may or may not be acting out of God's disciplining, but they will be mentors who are tasked with helping us, equipping us, and training us. They will aid in our seasoning and pruning.

Because of the mentors in my life, this process of growing and helping, and the one-on-one coaching I've received has helped to formulate the development of my why. I evolved into the person I am today because of the mentoring I received. That's why I seek to add value to people who in turn will add value to others leading to growth, transformation and changing this world.

As I have previously mentioned, there were two women who were instrumental in my adolescent years. Those two women were Jane Davis and Georgia Harris. Without either of them being placed into my life by the Father, I would not have followed the path that is the road for my life today. They were the "Moses'" in my life.

In my family, neither my mother or father finished high school; however, they were both hard working parents. My father worked for over 40 years for the railroad and served in the armed forces.

My mother was a stay-at-home mom. She was the homemaker, which is an important leadership role in every family. My mother was raised in the south and my father was raised in the north. Neither of my siblings had aspirations for college; thus I sought to follow in their footsteps. I attended John Marshall Harlan High School.

Each day for about a month I walked home with a folded sheet of paper and no books. The folded sheet of paper had the information I needed to study each night. I did not need my books. I would get home from school and go immediately to my room to read. Reading was my passion.

I previously mentioned how instrumental Jane Davis, my 9th grade gym teacher was in my life as a young adult. She became my mentor and was very impactful in my life. This is the story of my first encounter with her.

One day in her class, Ms. Davis called me out. She said "Shaheed" get over here." She called all her students by their last name. She said, "Every day I see you walking home with nothing but a folded sheet of paper in your hand. What are you doing with your life? Where is your homework? I told her that I completed my homework during breaks and lunch. I didn't need to carry books home. She said "What!?" and just looked at me.

Ms. Davis then said, " You are wasting your life away. What are your aspirations?" I told her I was going to follow my brother and sister and pursue a trade. I would be enrolling in home economics to develop that trade.

She immediately responded very adamantly, "No, you are not. Meet me in the Principal's office tomorrow at 8:00 am." I was like "Oh boy, I'm in trouble." However, I was far from being in trouble. From that day forward, she had me enrolled in Honor courses in high school. I graduated as Salutitorian in my class and was elected as Senior Class President.

Ms. Davis opened my eyes to see that I was more than what I believed I could be. Before Ms. Davis got hold of me; I had developed a preconception about myself. I was a product of my environment. I had developed a ceiling within my mind on how far I could go. I allowed my surroundings to dictate who I was and who I could become.

My environment was placing a lid on my potential and my capacity. She deprogrammed my mind, showing me that there was another way. I am forever grateful to her for changing the course of my life. I believe God placed her in my life to ensure I got on the path He intended for me.

The second instrumental mentor in my life I encountered in my Freshman year in College. I met Georgia Harris, the Vice President of a large pharmaceutical company.

Ms. Harris was a brilliant woman and a leader. I learned from her that leadership is not based on a position or title. No one has to appoint you to a position of leadership for you to lead. True leadership is seeing something that needs doing, and stepping up to do it. Leadership is valuing people and adding value to people.

This is nothing new. The prophetess Deborah said:

"When the princes in Israel take the lead, when the people willingly offer themselves—praise the Lord!" ~ Judges 5:2.

Now if you go back and read what Deborah was talking about, she was lamenting the fact that the men who should have made a difference and stepped up to lead were hanging back by the ships!

"Gilead stayed beyond the Jordan. And Dan, why did he linger by the ships?" (v. 17)

If you read Judges you'll see Deborah isn't upset that people were doing evil. She was upset they were doing nothing! How many of us come home and say, "I'm tired." And then we do nothing? Don't wait for someone to appoint you to lead. Find somewhere or something that cries out for a leader and lead. It doesn't have to be a big thing. And people don't have to see it and reward you. God sees. That's enough. In time people might notice, but we serve God and He sees all.

Because of Ms. Harris, I developed this same core value of leading where I'm planted, and it is a pillar in my life today. Ms. Harris also allowed me to work each summer at the company where she worked while I was on summer break from college. I could have stayed home and enjoyed my time off, but she was already impressing on me the desire to lead. She gave me an opportunity and opened my eyes to a world I had never seen — Corporate America.

She introduced me to a new way of life.

I gained confidence in myself, and in my capabilities. And I began to believe in my potential to become whoever I wanted. God gifts each of us with potential. Some are gifted more than others. It is our responsibility to use what he has gifted.

Let's go back to the Parable of the Bags of Gold in Matthew 25:14-30. We've talked about this once, but let's look closer at what happened:

"Again, it will be like a man going on a journey, who called his servants and entrusted his wealth to them. To one he gave five bags of gold, to another two bags, and to another one bag, each according to his ability.

Then he went on his journey. The man who had received five bags of gold went at once and put his money to work and gained five more bags.

So also, the one with two bags of gold gained two more. But the man who had received one bag went off, dug a hole in the ground and hid his master's money. After a long time the master of those servants returned and settled accounts with them. The man who had received five bags of gold brought the other five. 'Master,' he said, 'you entrusted me with five bags of gold. See, I have gained five more.

His master replied, 'Well done, good and faithful servant! You have been faithful with a few things; I will put you in charge of many things. Come and share your master's happiness!' The man with two bags of gold also came. 'Master,' he said, 'you entrusted me with two bags of gold; see, I have gained two more.' His master replied, 'Well done, good and faithful servant! You have been faithful with a few things; I will put you in charge of many things. Come and share your master's happiness!'

Then the man who had received one bag of gold came. 'Master,' he said, 'I knew that you are a hard man, harvesting where you have not sown and gathering where you have not scattered seed. So I was afraid and went out and hid your gold in the ground. See, here is what belongs to you.'

His master replied, 'You wicked, lazy servant! So you knew that I harvest where I have not sown and gather where I have not scattered seed?

*Well then, you should have put my money on deposit with the bankers,
so that when I returned I would have received it back with interest. 'So take
the bag of gold from him and give it to the one who has ten bags.
For whoever has will be given more, and they will have an abundance.
Whoever does not have, even what they have will be taken from them.
And throw that worthless servant outside, into the darkness, where there
will be weeping and gnashing of teeth.'"*

By not using what God has gifted us we are like the man who buried his gold in the ground. In essence we are stating we do not believe in His Word, or His generosity, or who He is. He is I AM.

He wasn't counting how many bags of gold each man had accumulated. The men were. The master was interested in how *faithful* they had been *to use* what they had been given — no matter how great, or how small it was.

It wasn't about the gold. It was about the *gift*. Have you been faithful with the gifts God has given you?

Both of these women showed me better ways to improve myself. They opened my mind up to a different perspective of myself and the world. God used these women to lay the foundation for who I have become today.

I'm sure I wasn't the only life they touched. Ms. Davis and Ms. Harris sharpened me and greatly added value to my life and the lives of others. Just as these women reached back to me. It is now my duty to do the same. Thus, I am committed to helping others, striving to touch a life and being impactful. I have reached back and will continue to do so. It is my call to be a servant and help to prepare, inspire, and motivate God's children.

I challenge you, dear reader, to do the same with your life. We must be willing to reach back and help others up. As we have been taught and continue to learn, we must be willing to show others the way and share what we have learned. The goal is to make each other better. We are not competing but completing. we are building others up to continue carrying the torch others have handed to us.

I don't know if you've ever watched the weeks and months leading up to the Olympic games or if you know the story about the lighting of the flame to start each Olympic games. A torch is lit in Olympia and a relay begins, with people running with the torch and passing it off along the way to the next person in the relay until it reaches its final destination: the Olympic stadium in the host city of the Olympic Games.

Once the flame arrives the last runner in the relay runs into the host stadium and lights the "Olympic cauldron" with the flame. That cauldron burns 24 hours a day for the duration of the games until it is finally extinguished at the end of the closing ceremony.

Each runner runs with a message of peace and purity. Thousands of runners have carried the torch over the last 100+ years, mostly by foot. While this ceremony is moving and inspires millions, there are other torches we don't see — the torch Christians pass along when they help, or disciple, or mentor others.

We need those behind us to continue the work that each of us started, and to pass God's torch to the future leaders.

As with Moses, we have to help raise and train up the future leaders of this world. If we fail to raise up future leaders, we will be like the Israelites after the death of Joshua.

They forgot for whence they came. They had no one to tell the story of their history and how God had delivered their ancestors from 400 years of slavery and gifted them with a Promised Land. It was the Promised Land that equipped them with the faith to continue growing and evolving.

But what happened? They lost their foundation and focus soon after entering the land. They became easily influenced by idols and others who were of the world.

You and I must not let the world win; we must fight the battle to train up others to take up the fight after we have passed away. We must fight for this world to become better, not staying the same or regressing.

We must believe in who created us and whom to which we belong in good times and in bad. Yes, it's the bad times that God uses to teach us to have faith in Him. He doesn't save us *from* the bad times.

He walks with us *through* them. That is how we learn faith. As we learn faith then we can help build up those with us and behind us.

Being Yoked

When I lost my brother to suicide, I was devastated. I had lost my best friend in the world. My brother was full of life; however, his life had to be a certain way. He could not handle the roller coaster ride that the journey of life entails.

Facing uncertainty, adversity and being uncomfortable was not acceptable. He did not understand that he was built to be an overcomer. He could survive and withstand, only he didn't know that.

When he died, I could not believe that he was gone. My grief was overwhelming. I isolated myself temporarily as I always do during times of a crisis to find my way.

I go within myself to reflect and gain strength. I lean on the Lord and His Word for guidance and support. Unfortunately, this time I latched on to someone that was not for me. He was not God's will for me.

This person was my first husband. In my grief I didn't look to God, but man. Yes, God provided me with all the signs that this was not the husband who He had selected for me. But I was not listening.

I ignored His talking to me and the signals He was providing. I kept seeing a green light when the light was RED. It clearly said STOP!

He had me return about five times, delaying our departure. I was like, "What is going on, I cannot get out of this house."

We eloped to Las Vegas, driving all the way. Prior to our departure, God attempted to stop me from traveling. He put up several obstacles in my path.

My soon to be husband acted like a maniac accusing me of cheating. I had a man at the house and he had just run out of the house.

I did not heed any of these signs. I kept going full steam ahead. I was thinking that I needed someone in my life after the loss of my brother. I said to myself, "God wants me to marry this person because I could help make him better. We could be a team. We can sharpen one another and build a solid foundation. He was spiritual, or at least he talked a good game about God, but God was not in him."

He was the strong man in Luke 11:25. The house had been swept clean on the outside but the inside lacked the presence and power of God. In my grief I was anxious to stop hurting and start feeling something besides that overwhelming pain.

I was willing to ignore God's signs, or twist them so I thought they were signs to proceed, just to escape my pain.

My honeymoon was the worst trip of my life. He was demeaning and treated me as if I was a bad person.

He accused me of hitting on his friend and being unfaithful to him. One day on our honeymoon he belittled me to the point that I sat in our room the entire day, crying.

The maid came into the room and attempted to lift me up and inspire me. I told her it was all my fault. She was very kind and attempted to console me. But I could not be consoled as I was seeking the affection and love of a man that didn't have it to give. His desire was not *for* me. His goal was to *control* me.

During my honeymoon, what should have been the happiest time of my life, was one of the worst times of my lfe. I was still grieving over the loss of my brother. The help mate who should have been my new husband should have been consoling and comforting me instead was nothing but abusive.

I was in a very vulnerable state. I was being beaten mentally by a husband, and suffering in anguish over the loss of my brother.

I endured the hardship of this marriage praying it would get better. Helped by this toxic man, I believed the lies that everything that occurred was my fault. I honestly believed that I needed to become a better wife and partner and help my husband overcome his issues.

Initially, I went to church with my husband. But like my marriage, I was not being fed. I was in the wilderness with nothing to sustain me. I would leave the church thinking, "what did I get out of this service? What did I learn?"

Each time, the answer was, "Nothing." I was empty. But God is faithful even when we don't see Him. He is always there. It took time, but God was finally able to wake me up.

The signs He had given me obviously weren't enough. So, He splashed cold water on my face.

I finally realized that the insecurities of my husband were his covering up his unfaithfulness and sinful behavior. The things I was being accused of were not about me but him. He wanted to control me so he could do all the sinful things he wanted while I suffered and cowered to him. After three years of marriage, I was finally seeing the light.

I've heard it said that first God will whisper in your ear. Then He will tap you on the shoulder. If you still don't hear Him, He will take stronger measures to get your attention. I liken it to a child walking towards a busy road.

At first the mother calls out to him saying, "Don't go near that road." If the child keeps on walking she then runs to him, stands in front of him and says, "I said, don't go near that road."

Finally, she will grab him by the arm and drag him back into the yard. She may even smack him on the bottom. God is our father.

He's not interested in stopping our adventure. He's intent on making sure we stay safe and follow Him.

Balaam's Donkey

It wasn't like God hadn't seen his children ignore very obvious signs they were on the wrong path. His desire is for us to be great. He knows what we are going to do before we are even in the situation.

Remember Balaam's donkey? Balaam was a wicked prophet, although not a false prophet. God did speak to Balaam, and gave him some true prophecies to share.

But Balaam's' heart was not right with God. And, he set out one day to betray Israel by leading them astray. But God stayed with him. We can read his story in the book of Numbers (22-24:25). Balaam gets up in the morning, saddles his donkey and goes to meet with the Moabite officials.

"But God was very angry when he went, and the angel of the Lord stood in the road to oppose him. Balaam was riding on his donkey, and his two servants were with him.

When the donkey saw the angel of the Lord standing in the road with a drawn sword in his hand, it turned off the road into a field. Balaam beat it to get it back on the road. Then the angel of the Lord stood in a narrow path through the vineyards, with walls on both sides. When the donkey saw the angel of the Lord, it pressed close to the wall, crushing Balaam's foot against it. So, he beat the donkey again.

Then the angel of the Lord moved on ahead and stood in a narrow place where there was no room to turn, either to the right or to the left.

When the donkey saw the angel of the Lord, it lay down under Balaam, and he was angry and beat it with his staff. Then the Lord opened the donkey's mouth, and it said to Balaam, "What have I done to you to make you beat me these three times?"

Now, if my donkey was talking to me, I wouldn't be yelling at him. I'd fall down with my mouth wide open in shock. But Balaam apparently didn't think a talking donkey was such a big deal, and it surely wasn't the voice of God.

Balaam answered the donkey, *"You have made a fool of me! If only I had a sword in my hand, I would kill you right now."* The donkey said to Balaam, *"Am I not your own donkey, which you have always ridden, to this day? Have I been in the habit of doing this to you?"*

Balaam thinks about this for a minute.

"No," he said. *Then the Lord opened Balaam's eyes, and he saw the angel of the Lord standing in the road with his sword drawn. So, he bowed low and fell facedown.*

The angel of the Lord asked him, "Why have you beaten your donkey these three times? I have come here to oppose you because your path is a reckless one before me.

The donkey saw me and turned away from me these three times. If it had not turned away, I would certainly have killed you by now, but I would have spared it."

Balaam said to the angel of the Lord, "I have sinned. I did not realize you were standing in the road to oppose me. Now if you are displeased, I will go back."

The angel of the Lord said to Balaam, "Go with the men, but speak only what I tell you." So Balaam went with Balak's officials.

When Balak heard that Balaam was coming, he went out to meet him at the Moabite town on the Arnon border, at the edge of his territory. Balak said to Balaam, "Did I not send you an urgent summons? Why didn't you come to me? Am I really not able to reward you?"

"Well, I have come to you now," Balaam replied. "But I can't say whatever I please. I must speak only what God puts in my mouth." Then Balaam went with Balak to Kiriath Huzoth."

Like Balaam, I eventually realized that I was heading down a path God didn't want me traveling down. I didn't get a talking donkey or an angel with a flaming sword to set me straight, but I did realize my husband's problems were not my problems.

I realized that *he* had to *want* to change. It wasn't up to me to change him. I will never forget what he said to me in an argument. He said, "I cannot break you."

I was amazed at these words. I guess you could say it was my "talking donkey" moment. I thought, "Wow, isn't this person supposed to be my other half and supportive of me. He is trying to break me."

I finally got fed up. I understood that God did not bring us together or want us together. It was time for me to move on.

During the four years of my marriage my cousin had become my sounding board. I thank her for patiently listening to me.

I know she was tired of my stories. They were entertaining, but I am sure she thought "When is this chick going to finally wake up?"

She would constantly say to me, "When you get tired, you will get tired and you'll know that you have had enough." Like Balaam, I wasn't ready to hear her. I would fight back with, "God brings man and wife together," to which she responded "God may not have brought the two of you together."

"What man brings together is not God's intentions."

After four years, one night of the same behavior became the turning point for me. My husband came home late, which wasn't normal in a marriage. but I had accepted it as the norm.

He would be out until after midnight or sometimes until 3 or 4 am in the morning. He woke me up, launching into me about cheating on him. This was the same old story. I had learned to be quiet when he preached it because I became fearful of the outcomes of these attacks during or afterwards.

This night, I did not think I was going to make it through his abuse without being seriously hurt. I was fearful. Throughout the night and wee hours of the morning, I prayed that God would protect me.

I would fall asleep in increments of about 30 minutes, waking up and listening to him again. He kept going on about me being unfaithful, and about my thinking he was stupid. Finally, I decided to get out of bed to get ready for work.

Hoping to get out of the house before this escalated into violence. I was ready to leave for work when the volcano erupted. He jumped out of the bed and knocked the TV mounted on the wall down.

A voice in my head said "Next it's going to be your head. Are you really going to continue in this situation?" I finally reacted. I said to him, "You have to go." If only it had been so easy to make him leave. He yelled back at me, "I'm not going anywhere!

I was in it up to my neck already, and it would only get worse if I backed down. So I said, "You have to go or I am calling the police." He didn't care. He said, "When the police arrive it will be too late to talk to me." I had had enough. So I called the police and he immediately vacated the premises before they arrived. Upon his departure, I changed the locks on the door and alarm code. Initially, during the separation, I thought we could possibly reconcile. That's a very common thought for women in abusive relationships. But God was with me.

He was leading me through the dark times whether I knew it or not. I didn't just separate from my husband. I left the church that wasn't feeding me either. I joined a new church and was baptized.

My Pastor was giving a Bible study on Married Life and being evenly yoked.

"God has called us to live in peace." ~1 Corinthians 7:15.

Then I realized there is no guarantee that he could save me or that I could save him. The scales were beginning to drop from my eyes.

Apostle Paul says it best in 2 Corinthians 6:14,
"Do not be yoked together with unbelievers."

Eventually I divorced my first husband because God was finally able to get into my thick head that this man was not for me. God did not bring us together. I did. I did not allow my first marriage to cause me to become bitter and hostile. I saw this as a lesson, an evaluated lesson. God brought me my second husband, David Jackson, who is my other half. We have become one in the way God intended.

"For this reason, a man will leave his father and mother and be united
with his wife, and the two will become one flesh." ~ Ephesians 5:31.

I have been blessed with a husband who has strong, deep roots that are deeply implanted in the LORD. He places God first in his life and follows His Word. God is in him. I thank God for blessing me with my husband. This union was His will and not mine.

Reflection
- Who are you mentoring?
- Who are you yoked with?
- How are you sharpening one another?

CHAPTER SEVEN

Self and Traveling Within

Every job I have held in life brought only temporary fulfillment. Without fail I would ultimately become discontent and restless. I would say to my sister my three favorite words — *"I am bored."*

My sister would say, *"I hate it when you say that. It means change is coming and things are going to start happening."*

I would just look at her perplexed and confused. Ultimately, she was correct. I would quit or get fired from whatever job I was working. Surely this was not God's plan?

I have continued to work all my life for others; however, working for others, being bored, this was not God's plan for me. I should have launched my own business years ago. I haven't done well working under others due to my free spirit and my restless drive to do better and to lead. Leadership was totally lacking in the companies in which I have worked.

Leadership in Corporate America was based on positions and titles when it should be based upon the people who were natural leaders, people who cared about serving the people on their teams and aiding in their development.

This kind of leadership builds trust and influence, not necessarily more money and a bigger office. I always compare the leaders I encountered to the two women who were instrumental in my life. They were sorely lacking in the passion and personal skills of my early mentors.

As such, I would become despondent and my performance at whatever job I was in would drop. I went from great to average or worse — often just barely getting by. I had no spark, no drive, and no inspiration, let alone the motivation to come up with ways to add value to the companies where I worked. I was living for each weekend.

In essence, I was rushing and wishing my life away. I would live for Friday. Then Saturday would rush by in a blur until the dreaded dawn of Sunday and promise of another long week at work. The entire day on Sunday, I was focusing on the fact I had to go back to work on Monday and wishing it was Friday.

It was like someone told me, "Time to get back in your cage." I would be filled with dread about Sunday ending. Monday would come and I would be in despair. Five more long miserable days lay ahead. And all I could think of was Friday, only to start the whole cycle over again.

During the approximately 35 years that I have worked, I have launched a couple of business ventures that did not pan out.

I wrote my first two books, *Reflections from Within* and *Messages from the Spirit*. God finally led me to joining the John Maxwell Team (JMT), leading to my becoming a certified coach, trainer and speaker. I have always had a drive to be self-employed; however, my fallacy was in believing I needed a safety net.

A safety net is an inhibition, enabling one to not take the risks to becoming better, but more importantly, not trusting in God. God takes our trust in Him, not in our own strength and might, very seriously. When God warned King David about "counting his army," He wanted David to know it didn't matter how strong his army was. It was God who fought his battles.

David didn't need to worry about whether he had enough men, swords, and horses to defeat the enemy.

But, as he always does, the devil noticed what was going. Just as he did with Adam and Eve, he moved David to disobey God and count his men. David, moved by pride and curiosity, took a census of his men and his armament. Unfortunately, what seemed like a simple census angered God because David, by counting his resources, could boast of his own power, not Gods.

And as a result God gave him three choices of punishment for his efforts: The first way was to have a famine throughout the land for seven years. The second choice of correction was to flee from his enemies for three months. David knew what this was like, as he had many times fled from Saul and even had to flee from his son Absalom.

The third way of being punished was three days of pestilence (a deadly epidemic) upon the land. David chose pestilence. Sadly, tens of thousands of Israelites died before David pleaded with God to stop the deaths. His pleas were heard and answered right before the death angel entered Jerusalem.

I don't think God has changed His mind about our not trusting Him. He wants us to trust Him. He craves our faith and trust in Him. It was another lesson I was to learn — that failure is not a sign not to move forward.

Prior to joining JMT, I had been coasting along trying different business ventures that did not pan out as expected. I had some clarification and focus; however, my *why* was not clearly developed. I would put in the work; however, I had to move, make sacrifices, and most of all, trust God.

I know that I am where I am supposed to be. God had to prune me and prepare me for the work for which He has predestined, but I was on the path. Since high school, I have always been passionate about writing and helping others. However, it took me about 20 years to put this talent to use. I initially started out texting to a small audience of close friends. I sent daily inspirational messages that blossomed into my writing books and a weekly blog.

My talents have continued to develop as I gained clarity and understanding in who I am and the why and what that I do.

Prior to obtaining my certification, I coached and mentored people for about 20 years. However, I did not see that this opportunity was my call to duty until I committed to the habit of intentionally growing and learning. My journey into growth began with my taking a Discipleship class at my church.

My pastor opened my eyes to understanding that every person has a calling. God will call us to duty if we're listening, looking, and trusting Him. Was I answering the call? This class opened my eyes to possibilities and opportunities God had planned for me all along.

I get fulfillment and joy helping others in their growth and development. I am thrilled when I see people blooming and seeing their potential, or changing their world and the world of those around them.

Within each of us is what we need to live a life of purpose. God sowed those gifts and talents planted within us.

What He requires is that we trust Him and tap into that which is within. This is our awareness of self. This is awareness of our strengths, skills and capabilities. We have the answers, but need to travel within.

James Allen says, "You cannot travel within and stand still without."

A man is what he thinks, what he believes is what he will become. You have to believe in *yourself* even when others do not. It is not about what others believe but what God believes and what He has instilled within you.

We hear about making our subconscious conscious. The subconscious is what controls our thinking and actions. The subconscious is your underlying beliefs in self and your abilities. We cannot allow fear and despair to hold us back from pressing forward, evolving, growing and becoming.

Fear and despair are distractions from the world. Did you know the Bible says, "Fear not" 356 times? Trusting God and turning from fear must be very important to be mentioned that often.

When the disciples asked Jesus questions, He said repeatedly, "Fear not." When the waves were crashing against the boat on the Sea of Galilee and the disciples were terrified and in fear for their lives, Jesus stilled the waves, then asked, "Why were you afraid?"

If God's word tells us to "fear not" that many times, shouldn't we listen? The enemy seeks for us to be distracted so that we will remain average, complacent, programmed, and fearful.

Distraction and fear lead to procrastination, giving up and settling.

What could you do if you were not afraid? What could you accomplish if you weren't afraid of failing, or of being rejected, or of humiliated, or being broke, or looking silly, or doing something everyone said you'd fail at?

If you notice, Jesus asked, *"You of little faith, why are you so afraid?"* Are you seeing the same pattern I'm seeing?

The lack of faith results in fear, and fear makes us take our eyes off of God.

Notice that once the Holy Ghost descended on the disciples at Pentecost, we didn't see fear much. The disciples were being beaten, tortured, and abused, yet kept coming back to preach the Gospel. What happened to these men and others who found a reason to banish fear from their lives? We're told we can do the same, so why don't we?

Know that God made you to be conquerors and overcomers. You were created with gifts, talents, and implanted with potential. Add God's command to "Fear not," and you have all you need to succeed.

We don't fight the battles ahead of us every day. God does. And He wants to! We're not asking Him to do something He dreads doing. He wants us to trust Him for His help and guidance.

This potential He's placed within each one of us allows us to pursue our purpose and live in the purpose He predestined us for. You and I have to obtain clarity on that which is within.

Our potential equips us to press forward. My participation in Discipleship class led me to join JMT, writing books and starting my company Faith, Hope & Spirit, LLC. I have found and discovered who I am and what I am to do. I am fulfilled and overjoyed with finding my purpose. Growth is vital to our life. It leads to transformation and changing our world and it pleases God.

Look in the Mirror

You must see value in yourself to add value to yourself and others. As the old saying goes, "You must love yourself before others can love you." Believe in the person in the mirror.

Ralph Waldo Emerson states what lies behind us and what lies before us are small matters compared to what lies within us.

Within each of us are the seeds God planted. He wants us to be successful.

"For I know the plans I have for you," declares the Lord.
"Plans to prosper you and not to harm you, plans to give you hope and a future." ~ Jeremiah 29:11.

God has placed the seeds that we must nourish so that they grow and bloom resulting in flourishing. We must be committed to sacrificing. Being persistent and consistent will feed the seeds to developing deep roots allowing us to pursue and fulfill our purpose.

God has intentions for each of us. It is our duty to answer and become what He envisioned for us.

His plan for our lives far exceeds anything we can imagine because He is God, the creator. He expects us to cultivate and grow, watering and feeding that is within.

Notice in Christ's parable about the owner who gave each of his employees bags of gold. He didn't tell them what to do with the gold. He trusted them to figure it out themselves.

He trusts us with the gifts and talents He has given us. He wants to see what we will do with our "gold." Will you invest your "gold" (gifts and talents) or will you bury them in the ground?

Where we fail is when we do not believe in self, not seeing the potential that is within each of us.

I say to each of you, look in the mirror believing in the person that you are. Believe in who you are and that which you can be. Don't listen to man (or women). They do not know God's will for you.

Wilma Rudolph was born premature in Clarksville, Tennessee. She was sickly, her family was poor and she was the 20th of 22 children.

She had polio, resulting in her having one crooked leg and a curved foot. Medical care was limited where she lived so she had to take a bus 50 miles from her home to receive treatments.

At nine years old, she decided to take the brace off her leg. She was determined to walk normally. She didn't give up.

Walking normally took her a few years to master. She knew God had greater plans for her no matter what her life was at the moment. Her faith, perseverance, tenacity and consistency became the things of legend.

Wilma loved sports, and she soon discovered that she had a joy for running. The girl who could barely walk became the woman who would one day run before Kings and Queens and the whole world when she went on to successfully compete in the 1956 and 1960 Olympics. However, she was more than an athlete.

Rudolph is also regarded as a civil rights and women's rights pioneer. She retired at the peak of her career in 1962. She was the world record-holder in the 100-and-200-meter individual events and the 4 × 100-meter relays.

A 1963 graduate of Tennessee State University, Rudolph became an educator and coach before dying of cancer in 1994. Do you still think God is hampered by circumstances? He knew you before you were conceived.

"Before I formed you in the womb I knew you, before you were born I set you apart; I appointed you as a prophet to the nations." ~ Jeremiah 1:5.

God is able to do anything He wants, so never doubt what he has planted within you and can do in your life. All that is required is that you believe in what has been planted within you. He equips us with what we need for our calling. We just need to answer when He calls.

Wilma said, "Running, at the time, was nothing but pure enjoyment for me. I loved the feeling of freedom... the fresh air, the feeling that the only person I'm really competing against in this is me."

Wilma was a woman born with physical deformities so great doctors didn't believe she'd ever walk, yet she became one of the world's fastest women, and one of the most successful and famous athletes of her era.

Her story is proof that each person is gifted by God with talent. We just need to get out of our way, let go of our fear, and claim what is rightly ours and daughters and sons of the King of Kings.

We get stuck because we don't believe in that which is within us. Will you put in the effort and time that is needed to develop and grow your talent? What if Wilma Rudolph had said, "Oh, I have a club foot. The doctors tell me I'll never walk. I guess they're all right."

I lost my brother at the age of 43. He did not see the person he was in the mirror. He did not know the person God saw. He was gifted with talent in information technology.

He built his own computer from scratch without any formal training. He had the knack for manufacturing and repairing computers. He did not see the gift and talent that was within him.

He did not see the potential and greatness that was within. I wonder if God wept knowing how his life would end, knowing the plans He had for him, to prosper him and grow him. God is our Father. He will not force or coerce us into following His plan for us. He wants us to trust him and seek His will.

As with my brother, there was an acquaintance, who I will call Thelma, who does not see the person *she* could be in the mirror. Her mother instilled in her that she was a slow learner. She placed her in a school for kids who had learning disabilities.

Not once was she tested to determine her educational level, or to see if she even had learning disabilities. Her mother programmed her to believe that her learning capacity was below normal. As such, she now looks in the mirror and does not see the value in herself, let alone her potential. Thelma has no desire to add value to herself. She has progressed through life believing that she is not worthy, believing that she is below average.

Due to her environment, she is a hostile and angry woman. She is antagonistic towards those who try to help her. Thelma has placed limits on herself. She has stopped growing, learning and expanding.

She has no belief in herself, or who she is and who she can become. Thelma refuses to water or feed the seeds within her thus life is going in only one direction – down. The decisions she makes hinder rather than empower.

I have and will continue to look at myself; the person in the mirror. I know who I am and believe in the greatness within me. I looked around my environment as I was growing up, but it wasn't until Ms Davis told me there was much more in me that I saw the light. I was the first to attend college in my family, thereafter progressing to earn a Master's Degree. From there I worked myself up the corporate ladder.

I became a leader who added to my leadership skills and development. I have been a leader serving within different organizations for over 30 years. I have held many titles which are not important because titles do not make me who I am.

Further, I have progressed to writing books, becoming a certified coach, trainer and speaker under the John Maxwell Team.

I seek to inspire and motivate others to see self and believe in themselves. My passion is to add value to others because I know we are all exceptional. We are not average or below average. Review these insights written by Edmund Gaudet. I challenge you to live your life by them:

- *Average is what the failures claim to be when their family and friends ask them why they are not more successful?*
- *"Average" is the top of the bottom, the best of the worst, the bottom of the top, the worst of the best. Which of these are you?*
- *Average" means being run-of-the-mill, mediocre, insignificant, an also-ran, a nonentity.*
- *Being "average" is the lazy person's cop-out; it's lacking the guts to take a stand in life; it's living by default.*
- *Being "average" is to take up space for no purpose; to take the trip through life, but never to pay the fare.*
- *Being "average" is to return no interest for God's investment in you.*
- *Being "average" is to pass one's life away with time, rather than to pass one's time away with life; it's to kill time, rather than to work it to death.*
- *To be "average" is to be forgotten once you pass from this life. The successful are remembered for their contributions; the failures are remembered because they tried; but the "average," the silent majority, is just forgotten.*
- *To be "average" is to commit the greatest crime one can against one's self, humanity, and one's God. The saddest epitaph is this' "Here lies Mr. and Ms. Average — here lies the remains of what might have been, except for their belief that they were only "average."*

I learned from my mother who stood for what she believed and believed in who she was. She was a strong woman of character and fortitude. My mother stood her ground and did not believe in backing down. Many people were fooled by her small stature because we tend to look at the outside rather than focusing on that which is within.

She was small in stature, no more than 4 feet 9 inches, but she was a leader.

As a child, my mother frequently referenced the quote by Martin Luther King Jr. *"a man cannot stand on your back unless it is bent."*

My back is not bent. I am standing straight and I will stand with you. We will press forward together. I believe in this person in the mirror as I believe in every person in this world. I will add value to you and you will in turn add value to others. Look at the person in the mirror and believe!

Know that in your race to the finish line, God has equipped you with what you need to run your race. You have gifts and talents. Use them to be of service in God's kingdom and join Him in the work He is doing. He is transforming this world and making it better.

Together we can make a difference with Him by being impactful and significant.

Turn Pain into Gain

The Law of Pain in the *15 Invaluable Laws of Growth* by John C. Maxwell says that, *"the good management of bad experiences leads to great growth and is necessary to grow. Pain is the darkness that leads to the dawn of gain."*

This law is tough for us to embrace because pain is something we seek to naturally avoid. However, this law teaches us how to turn bad experiences into positive actions that will lead to our being successful, growing and expanding.

We all have and will continue to have bad experiences. Bad experiences are a part of the journey of life. Most of the time when a bad experience dawns, we try to avoid the false reality by thinking that it did not happen, or wasn't our fault.

For me as well as you, we have had our share of bad experiences that have resulted because of our own actions. Prior to forming Faith, Hope and Spirit, LLC, I had the idea of owning an Edible Arrangements Franchise. This bad experience rates as number three in my top five of bad experiences.

I thought, "What an exciting business. I love fruit and I am an advocate of healthy eating."

For me, that thought alone should have been enough to warn me NOT to go into this business. It was not a good fit for me.

Just as with my first husband, I had every sign this was not a good venture for me. From the discovery trip to headquarters to learn about the franchise ownership until I signed the contract God was telling me, "No, no, and no."

But I didn't listen. This business venture culminated in my declaring bankruptcy and losing most of my savings. I partnered with a friend who also thought this was a good business venture opportunity.

First of all, the location of the franchise was wrong. We know that location is the key to business viability and sustainability.

. Next were the limitations on vendors. Franchise owners could only purchase products from the company's vendors, which drastically impacted my revenues. Prices were set and there was no room for negotiation to reduce costs.

This venture continued to spiral out of control due to the high costs of fruit and supplies. I could go on, but you get the picture. Eventually I was able to get out of the business after about five years.

This bad experience taught me two things: (1) pay attention to obstacles. Obstacles are signs that this venture or this person may not be the direction you should be traveling in.

Then, (2) do not throw good money after bad money. I was thankful for this experience which became an evaluated experience. It also led to honing my core values, passion and strengths.

This experience led to my developing my vision. Having a dream and a vision is instrumental to personal growth.

John McDonnell says, "Every problem introduces a person to himself."

This problem surely introduced me to myself. We all will have bad experiences. The bad news is, they cannot be avoided. The good news is, we learn more from our failures, mistakes, and suffering than we do from our wins if we allow ourselves to take responsibility for our mistakes and failures, and look at how we could have done better.

You are the one who chooses how you will handle the bad experiences as well as the good. You can choose to run, cope, drift along or embrace becoming better.

Bad experiences cannot be avoided and you shouldn't try to escape them. Pain leads to gain. We must choose to learn from difficult and challenging experiences. I don't know how many of you have ever worked out, or know someone who works out. But to grow muscle and strengthen bone you must tear down muscle and stress it.

I don't mean be so sore you can't move. But when bodybuilders and athletes go into the gym they're pushing their muscles to failure so the muscle will repair itself and become stronger and stronger.

God has created an entire universe based on failure. In 1991, an experiment in a glass dome enclosure called Biosphere 2 was started.

Scientists wanted to see how nature fared in an enclosed environment. What they noticed was that the trees inside Biosphere 2 grew very rapidly, more rapidly than they did outside of the dome. But there was a serious problem with the trees, and with many of the plants.

Before they were able to mature, they fell over. Now, there was no wind in the dome, nothing to stress the trees, or contribute to their failure—or so they thought.

After examining the trees more closely they discovered the lack of wind, or "stress" caused the trees not to develop something called "tension," or "stress wood." Apparently the trees needed wind and things that stressed them to develop the strength they needed to grow and thrive.

Think about a child who has an easy life versus a child who must work for what they get. Who will do better in life? A child who must do chores, is forced to work and study, or a child who has everything handed to them on a silver platter? Let's look at what the author of Hebrews had to say:

"And have you completely forgotten this word of encouragement that addresses you as a father addresses his son? It says, "My son, do not make light of the Lord's discipline, and do not lose heart when he rebukes you, because the Lord disciplines the one he loves, and he chastens everyone he accepts as his son." ~ Hebrews 12:5-6.

Paul was writing to Christians whose faith in Christ was being battered by strong Jewish influences. They were being persecuted for their faith in Jesus Christ. And it was getting old.

Can you understand how they might have been feeling? They were beginning to wonder if God loved or hated them. That's when they got this letter encouraging them and reminding them that they were being disciplined.

Life is filled with ups and downs. God never promised us a rose garden, but if He did, the roses aren't without thorns! The issue is most of us only seek to travel one way, UP!

God has not promised us a life with nothing but ease, good times, and boxes of chocolate. If this were so, we would not receive the seasoning and pruning that is required to become who we are intended. We must embrace the value of our bad experiences and learn to reframe them into positive thinking moving us forward. We must choose to not see failure but see ourselves as overcomers.

We must look at our bad life experiences as a resource to learn from and not as a setback. In life, we are winners and learners, not winners and losers. We are learners because we choose to learn from the pain using it to propel forward, lifting us up to soar higher.

Have you ever heard the expression, "Look for the silver lining?"

That means look for the lesson in whatever is happening to you, good or bad. If you have a flat tire, don't look at the tire, thank God it's not raining or freezing. If it is raining or freezing thank God you didn't crash.

There is always a silver lining in the darkest of clouds if you'll just look for it. If you can't see it, ask God to show you one. Not only will He gladly grant your wish, you'll grow closer because of it.

One of the biggest challenges from having bad experiences is making positive changes after learning from bad experiences.

"A bend in the road is not the end of the road...unless you forget to make the turn." ~ Author Unknown.

What happens to us is not the end of the road, it is a bend in which we must make a turn. Do not focus on your feelings but rather focus on your thoughts and actions which will lead you in a better direction. As an entrepreneur I can relate.

When a business hits a dead end a successful entrepreneur "pivots." That means they turn and go in a different and better direction.

Many of you use Twitter, or have heard of it. The same is true with Facebook.

Did you know both creators of these popular social media sites didn't start out with the platforms you see now? Both Twitter and Facebook evolved over time as the founders failed, and failed, and failed, yet learned from their mistakes.

My challenge to you is that the next time you have a bad experience, remind yourself that this experience is for you to evolve. Keep a positive mindset and thoughts.

Know that it will get better. Utilize and redirect your emotions to catapult you into changing, transforming and growing. Do not allow the bad experience to paralyze you creating fear which will stunt your growth.

As Roy T Bennett said, "Don't be pushed around by the fears in your mind. Be led by the dreams in your heart."

Reflection

- What do you see when you look within yourself? Who are you? Define who you are.
- What is the value that you see in yourself?
- Who are you allowing to devalue you? What actions can you take to stop allowing these individuals to devalue you?
- What lessons have you learned from your pain?
- How have you applied the pain in your life to living in your purpose?

CHAPTER EIGHT

Faith and Control

Who is in control of your life— you or God? Most of the things that happen to us are beyond our control.

What is within our control is our behavior, our responses and our actions. It's true, you are not to blame for a car running a red light and hitting your car. You are in control of how you respond to what happens afterward.

When Joni Eareckson Tada became a quadriplegic in a diving accident at the age of 17, she couldn't change what *had happened to her*. She could change *how she decided to respond* to the accident.

Before her accident she was active and on the go. She still is, but from a wheelchair. If that wasn't enough, she's also been through two cancer diagnoses. It wasn't an easy path and she's had her dark days, many days of depression and frustration.

She admits she was even suicidal, questioning God, and her faith. She was angry at the world, herself, and God. She didn't see any light in the dark tunnel she was in. But Joni found she had choices and influence.

To date she has written over forty books, recorded several musical albums, starred in an autobiographical movie of her life, and is an advocate for people with disabilities.

It took time — years. She got beyond her anger at God long enough to ask Him what His plans for her were. It was then a young man named Steve Estes came into her life.

He was not a love interest, but a friend. He was someone to be there for her, to work with her and deepen her faith in God. He was, as Joni says, *"...with me in my suffering."*

Joni has now been in ministry with her organization, "Joni and Friends" for more than 40 years. It may not have been the life she initially chose, but God had a greater vision.

That's not to say God has this kind of path for us all, but He does have a plan. So, stop trying to be in control of that which you are not. Let God do the work that is His. You do the work that is yours. Get in sync with the Lord.

"As the heavens are higher than the earth, so are my ways higher than your ways and my thoughts than your thoughts." ~ Isaiah 55:9.

God is always working around us. Our mission is to join God in the work that He is doing. We are to make the most of the light that is within us. Let your light shine brightly, living in your purpose before your light is extinguished.

"You are a mist that appears for a little while and then vanishes." ~ James 4:14.

In all that you seek to do, first consult God to see what it is that He wants you to do, and then listen to Him, even if you don't like what He's saying. He knows what is best for us. I had to learn the hard way about things that are outside of my control. I had to learn the lesson through my first marriage.

I had to learn the lesson from my failed franchise. It is not whatever I want. It is what God wants. We must be in alignment with what God wants us to do.

"Yet not as I will, but as you will." ~ Matthew 26:39.

It is what God wants for you not what you want. You may ask, but you may not receive. When you ask God, ask yourself why are you making this request? What are your motives? Is it to glorify the Lord or self? Your request must be in agreement with God and what He has predetermined for your life.

"If you abide in me, my words abide in you, ask whatever you wish and it will be done for you." ~ John 15:7.

This doesn't mean asking for a better car, better job, bigger house or a bigger bank account. The Apostle James writes:

"What causes fights and quarrels among you? Don't they come from your desires that battle within you? You desire but do not have, so you kill.

You covet but you cannot get what you want, so you quarrel and fight. You do not have because you do not ask God. When you ask, you do not receive, because you ask with wrong motives, that you may spend what you get on your pleasures."

God is not Santa Claus or an ATM machine to be tapped whenever we want something. God gives each of us what he wants us to have in accordance to our abilities.

He provides the resources for our journey. It is for us to take what He has provided, compounding and adding value for his glory and according to His will, not ours. I'm continuing to revisit the Parable of the Talents (Gold) in Matthew 25:14-15 because it is such a powerful parable. Each man was gifted talents based on his ability.

We have to be willing to put in the work which requires sacrificing, persistence and perseverance. God rewards his children. He wants each of us to be successful. Success is not based on things, what you have amassed or money.

Success is measured by the value you have added to God's kingdom and to others. You are to use your gifts and talents to be a servant. Do not think that you can ask for whatever you want and it will be provided.

You were created not for your own pleasure and selfishness but to be of service to the Lord. God gifts us with his image and Spirit to do his will. It is not your will.

Search your heart when asking God what you want. Is what you want for yourself and being used for the purpose of building up God's kingdom? Ask for what you want but ensure that it is in agreement with the will of God for your life.

"When you ask, you do not receive, because you ask with wrong motives, that you may spend what you get on your pleasures." ~ James 4:3.

After becoming a certified coach, trainer and speaker under the JMT. I would pray daily for God to bless me in my job. How selfish of me. I was not taking into consideration what God was doing or what he wanted me to do. God pointed me in the direction of becoming a certified member of the JMT.

I researched numerous other companies prior to JMT; however, God led me to this organization. After becoming certified, my thoughts were only on what I wanted; however, God gently stepped in and enlightened me. What I was, who I was and what lay ahead was not to give me what I wanted in this life, but what He wants me to do in His kingdom.

I must follow the Lord because He knows the way. My skills are to be used to build up *His kingdom*, helping others and adding value.

God has opened doors to me becoming involved in my local community as a Board Member of my local chamber, becoming a member of Toastmasters and joining non-profit ministries being a servant following the Lord.

Follow Me

Stop worrying about tomorrow, focus on today. Focus on what God wants you to do today. We are wasting time by not trusting Him.

We know that God is able to do all things and that with Him all things are possible. He has plans for you and me thus we need only to follow Him. In Matthew 4:18-20 Jesus saw James and John working with their father Zebedee. Jesus called them and they immediately left their father to follow him.

In Matthew 9:9, Jesus saw Matthew sitting at the tax collector's booth, saying to Matthew "Follow Me." Matthew got up and followed Him. In Acts 9:1-20, Jesus called the Apostle Paul to duty. Paul was on the road traveling to Damascus to further persecute the disciples and their followers. God got Paul's attention in a major way —blinding him for three days.

After the three days, his sight was restored and Paul at once began to preach the gospel in the synagogues to all who would listen to the news about the Son of God. Those who have ears let them hear.

In each one of these examples, each person followed the Lord, not asking any questions. They were not worried about the how and what because they had the Who. The same applies to each of us. We have the who (God) therefore no further resources or supplies are needed. What *is* needed is that we be obedient to answering and accepting His call. Just think if any of these men had worried about tomorrow, they would have missed the opportunity to be servants and to join God in the work He was doing.

Understand God is always working around us. It is for us to be invited to join and serve Him. We must focus on staying on the vine connected to our source.

Jesus said "I am the vine, you are the branches, whoever lives in me and I in him bears much fruit. However, apart from me you can do nothing."
~ John 15:5.

We are like the branches on a tree. When a branch is cut from a tree or falls off it no longer is able to live. The source of its life line has been removed or withdrawn. Jesus is our lifeline and He is sitting next to the Father interceding on our behalf. It is because of Him that we are able to have an abundant life, so never forget. We have the Who to which we need to follow and be obedient.

Matthew 6:33-34 says, "Seek first his kingdom and righteousness and all these things will be given to you as well."

Therefore, do not worry about tomorrow for tomorrow will take care of itself. Each day has enough of its own troubles. Reflect on the last time you worried. What did it change? Did it make a difference?

I have found that my worrying adds no value, it only results in me being distracted and distressed.

When we are distressed, it leads to us being distracted from what God wants us to do. We become disconnected which is what the world seeks for us to do. When our focus is off God, we are vulnerable to the schemes of the devil and his worker's taking us off our course.

We will lack energy, have no initiative and become focused. We become susceptible to negative thinking and doubting ourselves.

I recall a time in my career, where I was so focused and worried over my work situation that I was distracted from what I was supposed to be doing.

What is most ironic is that God was opening doors for me anyway. He was placing people in my life for me to connect and forge relationships with. People were seeking my services and skills through my company Faith, Hope and Spirit, LLC to perform work in my community and in their organization using my gifts.

However, I was continuously focusing on my negative work environment. My mind was consumed with negativity and worrying about tomorrow.

One morning, investigators arrived at my office questioning me about my using a USB cord that was in lost and found property.

The cord had been left unclaimed for over 120 days. I was using the cord to charge my cell phone at work. I was amazed. Once again it was like God had splashed cold water on my face.

I had been distracted by nonsense, and wasn't paying attention. I wasn't keeping my focus on the Lord. God had invited me to join Him in the work He was doing. He was calling me to follow Him.

Again, I wasn't listening. Instead, I was consumed with negativity about my work environment. I was allowing my work and negativity to control my mind and thoughts, not God. It was consuming me.

I was constantly focusing on how I was going to handle my supervisor. I did not need to handle anyone. God was in control and would handle the things and people that needed handling.

Once again, this situation occurred so that I would wake up. This same situation applies to all of us. Keep your focus on following God and listening to Him. He will take care of the rest.

Choose God and Choose Life

God IS! He is alive and active. He is a verb not a noun. As humans we have fear, discontent and anger due to adversity, trials and crises that occur in our life. We lose a job, or a loved one. We suffer injustice or are victims of violence. We tend to look only at ourselves as being the sole resource responsible for "dealing" with what has happened to us.

We forget that we have the strength of the LORD in our arsenal. We have limitations while God's power and resources are limitless. You are not able to "do all," but with God all is possible. He is the one who empowers and equips you to be able.

Everything is under God's control, occurring because of his reason and purpose.

Consider and meditate on the stories of Ruth and Esther. Both chose God and believed in His power. Ruth was not only poor, she had lost all that she had. She had no place to live or food to eat, but she became the ancestor of both David and Jesus. She chose God and life.

Esther was an orphan, but she became a queen who was instrumental in saving her people from persecution and extinction. In both examples, the women chose God and life. They chose to believe in HIM, not giving up on Him because of adverse life events.

Giving up wasn't an option for either of them. They both chose to press forward…

> "… forgetting what is behind and straining toward what is ahead."
> ~Philippians 3:13.

Understand that choosing God *will* lead to life, prosperity and success. You will not fail with God in control. God provides us with choices. It's what our "free will" is all about.

However, as I've learned through many of my choices, it isn't always easy for us to make the right choice.

It is easy to give into darkness because this is our nature. It's not that we say, "Oh! This is bad for me and I'm going to regret it, but I'm choosing it anyway."

The devil appears as an angel of light, and the sinful nature sees and wants an easy life, preferring immediate gratification and rewards over discipline, denial, and hard work.

Our flesh seeks the temporary short-term pleasures of the world because eternity is beyond our comprehension. Just because you are tempted does not mean that you have to execute or act upon the thoughts and feelings that come into your mind.

Know who you are and whom to which you belong. Think through your choices and decisions before committing to them. Trust God to lead you through things, knowing He has a plan to prosper you, not harm you. Don't mistake being disciplined for God's indifference to you.

God appointed Moses to deliver the Israelites from bondage and slavery in Egypt and to not only deliver them but lead them into a promised land of "milk and honey".

For 40 years God provided them with food, clothing and safety. They wore clothing and shoes that never wore out and their bellies that were always full.

For 40 years the Israelites witnessed the awesome power of God. God showed His strength and love for his people for decades.

The Promised Land could have been reached much sooner; however, the Israelites chose wrongly. They chose to believe in man.

In spite of the oppression and bad lives they'd lived under the harsh hand of Pharaoh, they wanted to return to Egypt, preferring being enslaved rather than following God. They preferred the tyrannical rule of Pharaoh rather than the light yoke of God.

After they had wandered bitterly, and aimlessly for 40 years, God gave them a Father to child talk. He laid down His rules for receiving the gift of the Promised Land. God offered the people two choices — life or death. Life and prosperity, or death and destruction.

"For I command you today to love the LORD your God, to walk in obedience to him, and to keep his commands, decrees and laws; then you will live and increase..." ~ Deuteronomy 30:16.

"Now choose life, so that you and your children may live and that you may love the LORD your God, listen to his voice, and hold fast to him."
~ Deuteronomy 30: 19-20.

He also promised them serious consequences for disobedience. (Read all of Deuteronomy 28:15-68 for the entire list.)

"But if you will not obey the voice of the Lord your God or be careful to do all his commandments and his statutes that I command you today, then all these curses shall come upon you and overtake you.
Cursed shall you be in the city, and cursed shall you be in the field.
Cursed shall be your basket and your kneading bowl.
Cursed shall be the fruit of your womb and the fruit of your ground, the increase of your herds and the young of your flock.
Cursed shall you be when you come in, and cursed shall you be when you go out. The Lord will send on you curses, confusion, and frustration in all that you undertake to do, until you are destroyed and perish quickly on account of the evil of your deeds, because you have forsaken me."

God is serious about sin and disobedience. The wrathful God of the Old Testament is the same loving God of the New Testament.

He has not changed. This same practice of choice and obedience applies to each of us today. We have the choice to follow God or disobey Him and follow the world. Following the world will result in living in darkness and ultimately lead to our destruction in every area of our lives.

Choosing a life of obedience will result in a life that is filled with the Lord's abundant love and promises, and ultimately to being blessed with eternal life.

We may not experience riches, abundance, and an easy life here on earth, but God has promised He will reward those who follow Him. Those who love Him with all their heart and soul, and have faith in Him will reap His abundance. You and I will have adversity and crises in our life. Obstacles, challenges and temptations are a part of life.

We will face times of uncertainty that will cause us to become resilient and stronger.

During adversity and uncertainty, you have two choices to withstand or fall. If you elect to fall it will provide a testimony to your strength.

"If you falter in a time of trouble, how small is your strength."
~ Proverbs 24:10.

History was made with the 2019 Government Shutdown. The shutdown, which lasted over 35 days, was the longest government shutdown in history.

Many government employees worked without receiving compensation. They weren't able to pay bills and many lacked the resources to provide for the basic necessities to sustain life, medicine, food, and more. Many turned to food banks and had to make the choice between reporting to work or lining up to get food from food pantries. Funds needed to buy gas were used to purchase food.

During the government shutdown, the politicians and the President were focused entirely on power and authority. Politics and political races outweighed taking care of the people they promised to serve if elected. It saddened me to see that the people in office who had promised their constituents that they would serve and protect, were failing to hold up to their promises, and were ignoring their responsibility. During this time of financial crises and adversity, one could have chosen to become bitter, angry and discouraged or chose to stay firmly rooted and planted in the Lord.

These kinds of crises aren't new. Throughout time God has used pestilence, famine, and power hungry rulers to get His people to focus on Him. God knows these things are coming and prepares a way for those who trust in Him.

Joseph, the youngest of Jacob's 12 sons, was almost killed by his brothers. That was their plan, but one brother convinced the others to instead sell Joseph into slavery. Joseph is eventually sold to Potiphar, the captain of the Pharaoh's guard.

There he becomes a servant, and an attractive man. Potiphar's wife notices this and repeatedly tries to seduce him. When she fails to seduce Joseph, she falsely accuses him of attempting to rape her resulting in him being thrown in prison on false charges.

It is generally believed that he spent 10-12 years there before interpreting dreams for the Pharaoh and getting back in his good graces. Joseph is then put in charge of collecting food in preparation for a coming time of seven years of drought and famine — making him a very powerful person in the Pharaoh's service.

From his position within the Pharaoh's service, he meets with brothers, and is able to reunite with them. Joseph gives them food, reassuring them their actions were part of God's plan for him to go to Egypt and save lives during the famine.

What we often fail to realize is our times of trial and testing, of difficulty and heartache may last for years, as did almost everyone in the Bible. God tests those whom He calls to serve Him: After fleeing Egypt after killing a man, Moses was a shepherd for 40 years before God appeared to him in a burning bush, calling him to lead the Israelites out of Egypt. Joseph was sold into slavery and spent 12 years in prison before being elevated to oversee the Pharaoh's food storage. As a young man David spent at least a year, if not longer, running from his best friend's father, King Saul, who was trying to kill him. His life was not easy, and his children included a son who tried to steal his throne and later murdered his brother who raped their sister.

If you read the Psalms you'll realize how depressed and down David often was. Job lost his children, his wealth, his livestock, his crops, his health and even the relationship of his wife and friends before God restored all he'd lost. He remained faithful to God, but he was desperately miserable at times:

- *"Why did I not perish at birth, and die as I came from the womb?" Job 3:11*
- *"I have no peace, no quietness, I have no rest, but only turmoil." Job 3:26*
- *"I loathe my very life, therefore I will give free rein to my complaint and speak out in the bitterness of my soul." Job 10:1*
- *"Terrors overwhelm me...my life ebbs away, days of suffering grip me. Night pierces my bones, my gnawing pains never rest." ~ Job 30:15-17.*

Elijah had great spiritual victories over the prophets of Baal, but then, when threatened with death from Jezebel, ran for his life, hiding in caves and being depressed and fearful.

There, in the desert, he sat down and prayed, defeated and worn, saying:

"I have had enough Lord, he said. Take my life, I am not better than my ancestors." ~ 1 Kings 19:4.

Other than John, every single disciple of Jesus met a violent and painful end, beheaded, crucified, or stoned to death. But John didn't have it easy. He was plunged in boiling oil, yet not scathed.

He was banished to the Island of Patmos where he lived in a cave where he received the vision he wrote about in Revelation.

Jesus, who was both fully man and fully God was also persecuted and crucified. Life is not for the weak. Yet, as Christians, God has equipped us to withstand what comes upon us, and promises to be with us through anything we must endure.

Jesus was born to be a sacrifice for our sins withstanding persecution, ridicule and being beaten. Jesus believed in the Father, choosing him over the world. He chose God and life. He did not give up.

Jesus remains dedicated and obedient to the purpose that his Father had predestined. As with Jesus, we must stay true to the calling for which we have created.

"As a prisoner for the Lord, I urge you to live a life worthy of the calling you have received. ~ Ephesians 4:1.

We are children of the Lord. We have his power and strength so we will not fall as long as we choose Him which will enable us to withstand.

"But we do not belong to those who shrink back and are destroyed, but to those who have faith and are saved." ~ Hebrews 10:39.

Depend on God

When your enemies are approaching, and it appears that their resources are greater than yours, remember the fight is God's, not yours. And God's resources most definitely exceed anything man can even imagine. Know that after the storm, you will have a testimony that will illustrate the love and mercy of God. When you are down and times are trying, that is the time when you need to lean on and look to the Lord. Set your anchor in him and hoist up your sails.

Each day you should be deepening and solidifying your relationship with the Lord, whether through times of plenty or times of drought.

During times of uncertainty, there are two key points that help you get through. One is to go deeper in Him and his word, praying and immersing yourself in the scriptures.

Secondly, look at where you are, and what you're doing. You may have lost your way; strayed from Christ and abandoned God, thus, you may need to return back to Him.

As we progress in our life, we need to go deeper into the LORD, not loosen our ties and our time with Him. Depend on the One who is able to be the warrior we are not.

God is the only One who can fight the battle that you cannot. We fail when we believe that we are in control of events and circumstances that are not under our control.

Recall the story of Jehoshaphat in which the vast armies of the Moab and Ammon were coming to wage a war against the people of Judah. Jehoshaphat called out to the Lord. He prayed to God, seeking the Lord's power and strength and God responded.

Battles that are greater than us, are not our battles to fight. The battle belongs to the Lord who has the power and strength to overcome what we cannot do on our own. The battle may be bigger than me and you, but nothing is too big for the Lord. The Lord responded to Jehoshaphat's prayers, saying:

"Do not be afraid or discouraged because of this vast army. For the battle is not yours, but God's. ~ 2 Chronicles 20:15.

The Lord delivered Jehoshaphat and his people from their enemies. The army of Jehoshaphat's enemy may have been vast; however, they could not withstand the power and strength of the Lord.

God had their enemies turn on one another causing them to destroy and kill one another. The people of Judah did not have to lift a hand, break a sweat or even lift up a sword or ax. What is even more ironic is that the people of Judah carried off all the equipment of their enemies, adding to their arsenal.

Know that God will use your enemies to fight and win your battles. He will deliver you. Just stand firm and believe. This story reveals to us that God has the power and strength. All that is required is that we lean into and depend upon Him.

Let me expand upon going deeper into the Lord. During my career, I was in a battle with those who were in authority, the senior leadership of the organization.

Each time they tried to form a weapon against me, God would come to my rescue. When battles are greater than me, the Lord has taught me to give them over to Him.

Do not take on that which is not for you to fight.

I recall one battle where a group of peers were brought in to investigate me. My supervisor felt that I was mismanaging my department. This was his chance to belittle my capabilities leading to my doubting who I am and *whose* I am.

The investigators were on-site for a week, interviewing all members of my team. After interviewing all team members, they reviewed the evidence with me to provide me with a summary of their findings.

The investigators determined that there was *no issue* with me. The issue was my supervisor who was not supportive of me as the leader over my department and valued the team as well as myself.

My supervisor was the one failing to assist me in meeting the operational needs of my department. They summarized that I was doing a good job running my department with the resources I was provided; thus, the issue was not with me. The report they provided was not favorable for my Supervisor. I was overwhelmed with God's mercy, love and grace. It reminded me of how Haman tried to have Mordecai and the Jews in King Xerxes's kingdom wrongly killed.

When Queen Esther told the king of the plot, King Xerxes was furious and demanded to know who had done this. He then had Haman hung on the very gallows he had erected to kill Mordecai.

The team who had been formed to harm me ended up like Haman, being the ones found to be in the wrong. God used them to deliver me. Instead of hurting me, they were helping me.

God will use that which is meant to harm you to be turned or used for your good. I no longer had any further issues with this supervisor attempting to attack me.

When the battle that was greater than me arose, God fought for me. The battle was too big for me, thus I gave it over to the Lord to fight for me. Know and believe that you are God's treasure and possession. He will take care of that which is bigger and greater than you.

Now let's look at losing our way or turning our back on God when we falsely believe that we are in control, or when we lose our humility and become self-seeking.

2 Chronicles 7:13-14 God says, "When I shut up the heavens so that there is no rain, or command locusts to devour the land or send a plague among my people, if my people, who are called by my name, will humble themselves and pray and seek my face and turned their wicked ways, then I will hear from heaven, and I will forgive their sin and will heal their land."

The COVID-19 pandemic of 2020 shut down the entire world. All countries came to a screeching halt. Prior to the pandemic, Democrats and Republicans were constantly bickering, losing sight of why they were elected into office.

Our politicians are appointed to serve and protect the people. Instead, they were focusing on their own agendas. From 2016 to 2020 crime continued to escalate. Man fighting against man and man killing man.

There was no appreciation for the gift of life. Racism and vandalism of the churches soared, along with people killing people in the churches. The church is a sacred place; however, mankind did not see or comprehend this sacredness.

Finally, the poop hit the fan, splattering saints and sinners alike. No one was immune to the killing, the hate, and the crimes. While no one was watching or paying attention, the virus was allowed to penetrate and take root in our world.

Understand, I do not believe that God created the virus but he did permit it to occur. Mankind needed time to pause, reflect and reset. Many of his children have lost their way and have turned their backs on God, preferring to concentrate on self-gratification, being prideful and self-seeking.

COVID-19 was a catalyst for unification. People came together seeking to make a difference, be impactful and add value to this world. We have to believe and know that out of bad can come goodness.

Romans 8:37 states, "And we know that in all things God works for the good of those who love him, who have been called according to his purpose.

God uses discipline to bring us back to Him so we can realize who we are, find our purpose and answer His call. We lose focus when we become disconnected from Him. We are like the Prodigal Son who embraced the world, then realized what he wanted and needed was his father's love. We must return to God, our father, and our Provider.

Withstand

There will be times that you must make the choice to stand your ground. You must be willing to withstand the fire before you, believing that God will take care of you.

You may be placed in the fire but the fire will not harm you. In the Book of Daniel, three men (Shadrach, Meshach and Abednego) stood firm on not worshipping or bowing down to an idol.

King Nebuchadnezzar made an idol, issuing a decree that whomever that did not fall down and worship his idol would be thrown into the fiery furnace. God issued the ten commandments to be the guiding principles for our life.

God said, "You shall have no other gods before me. You shall not make for yourself an image in the form of anything in heaven above or on the earth beneath or in the waters below.
'You shall not bow down to them or worship them; for I, the LORD your God, am a jealous God." ~ Exodus 20:3-5.

As you journey throughout your life, man will try to get you to turn from God and to the things and pleasures of the world. Man will seek to entice you to worship him and want you to think that he is in control, just like Nebuchadnezzar.

You will need to make the decision to stand your ground and withstand the temptations —because there will be many. The devil will not be content until he has stolen, misdirected, and claimed as many of God's children as he can.

My job went through a realignment resulting in a downsizing and shifting of my responsibilities.

My supervisor would continually say to me, "I am trying to save your job and all the others in your department." I would continually look at him, thinking "it is not under your control. God is in control."

God has already predestined what is to occur in my life. I just need to follow Him. If it is God's will, the job would not be eliminated otherwise He has determined that it is time for me to move on to where He needs me to be.

I know he was just trying to be reassuring, but I was not going to bow down and worship man, who was not in control. My supervisor was in and of the world.

Like many believers and nonbelievers, his thinking was delusional.

He truly believed he was in control and that he, not God, had the power to control the lives of others.

God uses man, both believers and non-believers, to do his bidding thus we are all instruments of the Lord. Man cannot control the journey of his life, let alone the lives of others.

When we think we have our hand on the fate of ourselves, our children, our family or friends, we are sorely mistaken. The best we can do is pray for those we love, not tell them what to do or not to do.

"The prayers of a righteous man availeth much, if it be fervent."
~ James 5:16.

God utilizes His wisdom and omnipotence to steer his children along their journey. We don't need to worry, indeed God tells us not to worry. He is in control. Shadrach, Meshach and Abednego say it best:

"If we are thrown into a blazing furnace, the God we serve is able to deliver us from it, and he will deliver us from Your Majesty's hand. But even if he does not, we want you to know, Your Majesty, that we will not serve the gods or worship the image of gold you have set up." ~ Daniel 3:18.

I know that God is in control of my life and that with Him I can withstand anything this life or the devil throws at me. I had been on my job for over 17 years and was closing in on my retirement.

One would say not getting to 20 years is a bad thing, but it is God's will not mine. He is the pilot of my life.

I do not put my faith in man, I will keep my faith in the Lord. The One who can and will make the impossible possible.

God says "Because he loves me says the Lord, I will rescue him; I will protect him, for he acknowledges my name." ~ Psalm 91:14."

Hold steadfast to your faith and to the Lord. Follow the purpose for which you were created. Do not allow anyone to deter you, turning your mind to thinking that a man is in control.

The more you trust God, be aware the more likely it is that both man and the devil will become jealous of your solid foundation. They will attempt to shake your faith. God has the power and not man, and not the devil. Man will try to steer you from God and attempt to influence your mind. Man seeks to program your mind to believe that he is in control and has power over your destiny. He is jealous of the rock from which you are cut. The rock that is the foundation of your life is the Almighty God. Don't forget that.

Man, who is in and of the world cannot understand the power and strength of your foundation. They cannot wrap their brains around the Creator we serve. King Nebuchadnezzar was amazed at the strength of the faith of Shadrach, Meshach and Abednego.

It was their faith that caused them to turn to God. He witnessed the power of God. He saw the power of unshakeable faith and obedience to the Lord. He surely thought that they would turn from God after he threatened to throw them into a fiery furnace.

To make it worse, he heated the furnace seven times hotter than usual. He was thinking, "I know I am going to make them turn from God."

He thought, "I am going to show them who is in control and has the power." He thought, "Their Almighty God could not be greater than his idols." I still see this attitude in man, and women today. King Nebuchadnezzar however, received a wakeup call, an awakening to the power of the Lord.

The men were thrown into the furnace with their hands and feet bound. But the only thing that was burned was the ropes binding their limbs. Not a hair on their heads, their skin, or the clothes on their bodies, were singed or burned by the fire. There was not even a whiff of the smell of smoke on them! God had sent His Son to protect the men. King Nebuchadnezzar was amazed, he said:

"Look! I see four men walking around in the fire, unbound and unharmed, and the fourth looks like the son of the gods." ~ Daniel 3:25.

Thereafter Nebuchadnezzar said "Praise be to the God of Shadrach, Meshach and Abednego. After what he witnessed, Nebuchadnezzar became the biggest champion of God. He not only converted but instructed his entire kingdom to follow God.

Nebuchadnezzar recognized and respected the power that he had witnessed of the Lord. He was a first-hand witness to the fact that idols were insignificant and worthless. God was Almighty. With Him, you can withstand.

Reflection

- What are you asking God to do in your life? Why are you making this request?
- Who are you following, man or God?
- How does your life reflect who you are following?
- What situations have you made a stand? What was the outcome and impact?
- Have you considered sacrificing your values for God? Why?

CHAPTER NINE

The Overcomer | Look Up

Y ou and I are overcomers. *"In all these things we are more than conquerors through him who loved us." ~ Romans 8:37.*

God did not create us to be conquered but to be conquerors. We are overcomers. The pandemic of COVID-19 has been a hard time for all of mankind. Many have been hurting financially, spiritually, emotionally and physically.

We cannot allow a pandemic to win over who we are. This should not come as a surprise however. God told us in the end times there would be pandemics, pestilences, and famines. He also promised to be with us through it all.

Know that out of pain comes light and greatness. We have to sacrifice in order to become better, unleashing the potential that is within.

Nothing worth having in life comes without trials, storms and pain. Believe that what is waiting on the other side is worth the pain we experience today. This is easier said than done; however, we must focus on what can be instead of that which is.

Know and believe that the circumstance and the situation shall pass, leading to better and greater. During these times, we are being molded, adding to our character. We are being equipped and being prepared for that which we must do. You and I must never give up on hope.

"Hope never abandons you, you abandon it." ~ George Weinberg

My pastor shared this message with me, and I share it with you. Look up, not down. For when you look up, you see stars and hope.

When you look down, you see dirt and mud, leading to despair and distraction. Know that despair and distraction is what the enemy seeks for you. His plan is for you to become so despondent and distracted that you will not be a conqueror. He wants you to give up.

Know that giving up is not an option. You must press forward, to a new day, knowing that better times are on the horizon.

Recall the stoning of Stephen, the first Christian martyr. Stephen had great faith in the Lord and great influence among the people. Jewish leaders fearful of his influence seized him to persecute him. Stephen was not afraid.

He said, "Look I see heaven open and the Son of Man standing at the right hand of God." ~ Acts 7:56.

Stephen looked up, seeing hope and glory. Thus, like Stephen, look up and not down, for our God is forever present and working. You and I are conquerors because of hope and faith in God.

Blow Up Normal

Normal is a setting on our washing machines. It's certainly not much of anything else. So, let us discontinue using the word normal.

Normal is what we have developed and been programmed to believe is the only way to be. Normal is average and uninspiring. Normal is our way of becoming complacent and settling for things we don't need to settle for.

We must embrace the future that is before us and aim to soar higher. We have not reached an end of the road, only a bend that requires that we each make the turn. Uncertainty requires us to blow up on the box on our "normal."

During times of uncertainty, take the time to pause and reflect, getting to know yourself. Take inventory of your skills and capabilities leading to developing and enhancing your why.

What is your cause? What is your passion? Your cause is your passion, that which drives you to be better. Each of us must not settle for being average but better.

Within you there is greatness, thus you will overcome times of uncertainty becoming better. Do not give up on, instead focus on the possibilities and opportunities. Be prepared for new opportunities that will be revealed thus you must equip yourself and be ready to take action. Always have hope for a better day, a better tomorrow.

Remember hope does not abandon you, you abandon it. Believe in that which is within you, embracing the tomorrow that will come filled with new opportunities.

Don't look back on yesterday, and don't long for the old way of life. Remember the Israelites? They looked back and longed for the old days of Egypt.

Lot's wife looked back with longing for the past, and turned into a pillar of salt. Don't look back. Embrace the new, the better, the future God has planned for you.

Life is a progression; we do not stand still. We are continually evolving and transforming. Always, look forward to becoming better and having better.

The Israelites were content with being slaves to the Egyptians because this was their normal. However, they were settling to be below average and not believing in better. Each day is a new day filled with possibilities and opportunities that we are to embrace and seek. God is not normal thus neither are you. Each of us is challenged with continually renewing our mind, focusing on being better each day. Let us stop searching for normal and instead search for better.

However, normal is not what God has determined for us. There is nothing normal about God, thus neither is there anything normal for you to settle for.

We must be willing to shake up, unsettle our life in order to get and receive better. The Israelites didn't like being enslaved to the Egyptians, but it was comfortable.

They knew what to expect, even if it was beatings and horrific working and living conditions. That, they thought, was better than facing a new life with new challenges. They wanted to be in control. They wanted reassurances. They had become complacent to being slaves.

Moses said,"Do not be afraid. Stand firm and you will see the deliverance the Lord will bring you today. The Egyptians you see today you will never see again." ~ Exodus 14:13.

Thus you must be willing to give up that which is normal to receive that which is different, and better. With change comes the distractions of anxiety, depression and despair. The Israelites didn't like change. Not many of us do. They were called out of their comfort zone by God Himself, and within days were regretting their decision.

Do you give up as easily? They were all excited to be leaving Egypt, but when the reality set in, and the heat, the hard times, the different camp setup every night began to wear on them, they began to grumble.

Isn't that what happens to so many of us? We start off excited with the newness, but when things get hard, we grumble. Stop grumbling. Know that you are an overcomer.

You were gifted with this life, and the talents and skills God gave you to go out and add value to this world. We each have a purpose. We were each provided the gift of life because we are conquerors. Thus, blow up normal, embrace the unknown, and forge a new path becoming better with each day.

Stop looking in the rearview mirror and start looking forward..

Your Testimony

In your life you will encounter and withstand many experiences, crises, trials or storms. You will suffer setbacks and disappointments, however, rejoice in your having endured and persevered through them.

Do not allow your experiences, good or bad, to hold you back. Develop a deep and full relationship with the Lord, knowing that he is God and the Lord of your life.

He created you and knew you before you were conceived. He has counted all the hairs on your head. He is a Sustainer, a Healer, and our Redeemer.

You have endured because with Him, all things are possible. You have a testimony, which is your duty to share. You have the responsibility to train and lift up future generations. Be a mentor.

You are responsible for creating the future leaders of this world, and training the next generation to add value to the world and each other. You are the light and beacon that provides light to others. You don't have to be perfect before you start. Moses learned how to lead along the way. You will too.

Each of us has a testimony — our compilation of trials, storms and tests in your life. I call these our scars. And as they say, "Every scar tells a story."

Your faith will be tested and pain is a part of life. The key is how you handle your tests and how you deal with the pain. Our storms, trials or hardships are for us to endure and withstand, to build the resilience that adds to our character and builds our strength. Your testimony is about how you become who you were created to be, how you learned how to fulfill your purpose.

Don't be ashamed of the trials, hardships, storms and pain that led to clarifying your purpose, or developing your skills/trade, helping others and strengthening your relationship with the Lord. Your testimony testifies to the love, mercy and grace of the Lord. Your testimony may be very painful.

The pain is what makes it powerful not shutting us down but building us up to share with others. Ask yourself, how do you plan to use the experience?

John McDonnell says "Every problem introduces a person to himself."

Each experience you have allows you to get to know yourself better, realizing the strength and power that resides within you.

"But we do not belong to those who shrink back and are destroyed, but to those who have faith and are saved." ~ Hebrews 10:39.

You have a testimony that God wants you to share. Your testimony will help another, you will be a light to them in their darkness as others have been a light to you. You will provide them with inspiration and motivation to continue pressing forward when they are down.

Your testimony will show the solidity of your faith, love and hope. Others will see how you endured, adding to your character and strength.

"Because we know that suffering produces perseverance; perseverance, character; and character, hope." ~ Romans 5:3-4.

You are not alone in sharing your trials and challenges. In 1 Corinthians 4, the Apostle Paul describes the hardship and suffering of the apostles. They were hungry, thirsty, naked, homeless and laborers; however, they never wavered. Even Jesus was hungry, tired and challenged.

The night before he was arrested Jesus prayed that if it was at all possible, that God would take this cup (His crucifixion and the death that laid before him) from Him. But God had a plan, to redeem all of mankind. Being weak, being persecuted, being tortured is not a reason to hide or remain silent.

As Paul said, "We have become the scum of the earth, the garbage of the world-right up to this moment." ~ 1 Corinthians 4:13.

Through all the abuse, being laughed at, beaten, whipped, and stoned,, the apostles withstood it all, understanding their purpose was to spread the gospel. They created a testimony which is still being told and read today. The testimony of each apostle provides each of us with hope, knowing if they can endure so can each of us.

As we share our testimony, we add value to others and to God's kingdom. We inspire, motivate and give hope to people feeling certain they can't go on. Each of us is tasked with helping one another, with being a servant to our brothers and sisters. Most importantly we are tasked with loving one another.

It is through the love, grace and mercy of God that you were created and have life. It is because of God's grace that our sins have been forgiven and the sting of penalty has been cancelled.

God has gifted us with grace through his son, Jesus.

Your pain and trials are a compilation of your testimony. Whether you know it, or believe it or not you have a testimony that may be more or less difficult than another; however, it is your story. It's not a competition. God gives each of us that we can bear and provides a way out.

Your testimony, the things you have endured or fought through have molded you into the being who you are today, which is continually evolving. We will forever be on the potter's wheel.

Be thankful and praise God, for the molding. Share your testimony, help another person, add value to this world and another, providing inspiration and hope.

"Your story could be the key that unlocks someone else's prison. Don't be afraid to share it." ~ Author Unknown.

Hope

Life requires and dictates that we encounter adversity. Remember the trees and the "stress wood" which made them stronger and more capable of standing through a storm?

Our adversity is the thing which makes us stronger, and prepares us for who we are to become. We must not be conquered but victorious. God did not make us to roll over and give up. He created us to have endurance, perseverance and tenacity. We (you and I) cannot lose sight of hope.

"But hope that is seen is no hope at all." ~ Romans 8:24.

Hope is believing that a certain thing or situation will happen. If you believe it can happen, it will. We cannot see hope but we know that it exists.

It is intangible but forever present. It is on the horizon just like the sun that may not always come out but it is there, just hidden by the clouds. With trials, there will be obstacles and hardships; however, the key is to not allow them to overcome you, but to learn from them.

In the second year of my marriage to David, my second husband, we endured a financial hardship that lasted about eight months.

I was amazed at the quickness in which we encountered our first test. I thought we would have a honeymoon with roses and chocolates for about five years; however, this was not God's plan. David was suspended from his job due to a resident making a false allegation against him.

At the time, the policy for his job was that you were guilty unless the evidence proved differently. I was amazed. We had two car notes and had recently acquired a few extra bills from performing renovations around the house. Further, this suspension occurred around the Christmas holidays so any plans we had for a vacation were nixed. His suspension progressed through the middle of summer.

Eventually, David sought temporary employment. We had to find another source of income. We had to find another way; one way is not the only way. We had to open our mind, deprogramming ourselves from the notion that a specific way is the *only* way. I was thankful for David's mindset of not just drowning in self-pity but instead seeking to come up with solutions.

God answered our prayers. David was able to secure another job after two weeks of searching. Even if I thought at the time that David wasn't the man I was supposed to be with either, God was answering our prayers, seeing that we were in need. He was behind the scenes working and providing.

I could see my husband was suffering. He thought he had failed our household and that he was at fault. It was hard for me as well. I was the primary breadwinner and I was carrying the weight of keeping us afloat. In addition, I had just launched my new business, so we were deep in debt.

My job was stressful. I was dealing with a supervisor who was about self, who was disrespectful and dishonest. I was overwhelmed and being mentally drained each day. I considered giving up on my business. I felt we were being punished and I sought God for the answer.

This period of adversity pressed home to me that that marriage is a union where God must be first. Marriage requires God to be at the head, leading and guiding. David and I were a team that required our marriage to be anchored in God.

God had to be first and the rest would follow. Further, I knew that our trials and storms in marriages are sent to solidify the union. The purpose of our storm was to build up not tear down.

You and I cannot allow the trials and storms to sway or distract, resulting in losing our hope or the light and spark from our life.

No matter what, we must stay the course, forging ahead knowing that better times are coming. This is hope. Storms and trials don't just build our character, they reveal our character and our strength.

The Apostle Paul said, "Because we know that suffering produces perseverance; perseverance, character; and character, hope." ~ Romans 5:3-4.

Hope is vital to our survival. We must have and believe in hope. We must believe that Hope is attainable and will come. We must believe that with faith, Hope will come to pass.

Hope will cause the storm to pass. Hope believes that being better is achievable and attainable. Better is the outcome of storms and trials when we have Hope. God's word is true. He did not create us to cower and be failures. God created us to succeed, to have a future that is filled with potential and possibilities. It is up to you and I to believe. During this financial storm, David and I never lost hope.

We knew that God was going to deliver us, returning him back to work. We just had to wait for God to provide, which He did. Ultimately, David was exonerated and returned back to work after 8 months. This trial also showed me that the potter's wheel is a constantly evolving process.

God is never done with us; we are continually being molded and sculpted into what we need to become for the assignment that is waiting for us. Our life is based on stages and levels during which we will endure and withstand trails and storms, periods of adversity. When God is done with us our character will be stronger and we will be prepared for the next season of our lives.

Do not fret and do not grow weary. Love and worship God during storms and trials and do not be angry or distressed.

"May the God of hope fill you with all joy and peace as you trust in him so that you may overflow with hope by the power of the Holy Spirit."
~ Romans 15:13

Crises in Life

We will experience crises in our life. That's just how a life with a sin nature works. Crises are defined as difficult times when we become distressed and distracted. Normalcy is shaken and your way of life is turned upside down.

Know that comfortability and complacency will not lead us to who were created to be or where we need to go.

Crises are part of the journey of life. We will be unprepared; we will be afraid because with God there is no advance notice. There will be no warning which is why we call it a crisis. What will be instrumental is how you deal with the crisis, not whose fault it is, or whether or not you did something to deserve it. Don't focus on blame. Focus on Faith. John Maxwell says, *"Feed your faith and starve your fears."*

The disciple Timothy says, "Fight the good fight of the faith."
~ 1 Timothy 6:12.

Faith doesn't lessen the crisis; however, it allows you to withstand it, to trust God to walk with you through it, and it strengthens us and pleases God. We must also have hope — believing in better things for tomorrow. Tomorrow *will* be greater and better. We must be willing to give up to make room for exceptional. My Pastor recently gave a message that resonates within me. He said:

"Look up, see the stars which signifies hope. Look down, you will see mud and dirt which signifies despair and distress. Now faith is confidence in what we hope for and assurance about what we do not see."
~ Hebrews 11:1.

Do not look down, look up. Better is always possible and will come. God is a deliverer, a redeemer, a healer and a provider. He takes care of his children. Have faith knowing that you can rebuild and overcome.

To get better, requires going through the crisis and sacrificing. You cannot focus on going back to that which once was, instead you must go forward. The purpose of the crisis is to have you shed those things or people that are holding you back from what is to come.

The Apostle Paul says, "Let us throw off that which hinders and the sin that so easily entangles." ~ Hebrews 12:1.

We can get stuck on normalcy. Normalcy is a hindrance to our seeking to become better. We become accustomed to things in life because we are satisfying the flesh and not feeding our spirit. We live for the Spirit not the flesh.

We cannot remain focused on the past and things of the world; they will stop us from moving forward. God has a plan for each of us, which is to be impactful and significant. We are to add value to His kingdom, His children and serve Him.

Reflect on Abraham, Isaac and Jacob and others. All left behind that which was comfortable following God.

"If they had been thinking of the country they had left, they would have had the opportunity to return. Instead, they were longing for a better country—a heavenly one." ~ Hebrews 11:15-16.

Do not long for what has passed, embrace new and better. Believe that out of bad comes good. We each are on the potter's wheel being molded to fulfill the purpose for which we have been created.

The crises in our life are allowed and occur to build character which equips us to perform the assignment for which we have been called.

As with you who are reading this book, you have had to ensure crises that have only made you stronger and better.

We will suffer for doing good because that's how life is.

Life, good or bad, happens to the good and the evil, the believer and the non-believer. You must believe in who you are and have resilience because God has a plan for the crises that happen to us all.

In March 2020, the COVID-19 pandemic occurred, shutting down the entire country. The pandemic held the entire world hostage.

A vaccine had to be developed and administered, allowing the world to develop new ways of living and doing business. Mankind will forever remember this crisis, reflecting on the impact on their lives. Life as we had known, had been uprooted and came to a halt.

Churches, businesses, major corporations, airline industry, schools, colleges, universities, parks, etc. were all shut down due to states enacting Shelter in Place mandates. Life as we knew it had come to a halt forcing many to pause and reflect. Going back to basics.

If this was not enough for me to handle, I was being attacked on my job by those who were jealous, greedy and prideful. I felt as if my world was crumbling. I was becoming overwhelmed with sadness, leading to my being distressed. During this time, I choose to lean on God and His Word.

I know that God did not bring me this far to have me turn back or to abandon me. I saw Him working in my life and I witnessed His power. Each time I was attacked He provided a response and delivered me. One particular incident stands out in my mind.

One afternoon in the middle of the COVID-19 pandemic, I was questioned by internal investigators regarding misuse of lost and found property, specifically a USB cord that I utilized to charge my personal cell phone. I've mentioned this before, and I do so now because after all this time, the shock of what happened still affects me when I recall it.

I was speechless. Now understand, cords are customarily tossed in the trash or recycled thus this is not property of any real value and is not normally returned to any customer. Thus, you can see my amazement. My integrity and job were being placed on the line for a USB cord that had been abandoned in lost property. I reflect back on many occasions where I had used the charger for my personal phone to charge my work phone; however, this was acceptable.

I thought of all the serious, deadly, horrible things going on in this world, and these people had time to question me about a borrowed phone charger.

I was angry and amazed. However, God showed me His power, after some research they learned that the USB charger that I was using was not lost and found property; it was the property of a coworker who worked in the Lost and Found Property Office.

This was a wakeup call for me. I had been sleeping. I had lost sight of the fact the enemy is always seeking to kill and destroy. Thus, I needed to remain vigilant and get back my focus. I had lost sight of what I was to be doing, getting better through the crisis, overcoming and getting to the other side.

Crises are our wake-up calls. We have become comfortable and complacent, leading to hindering growth and progress. You have to believe that you will rebuild, recover, adapt and most importantly be transformed. You must feed your faith and starve your fear.

Faith is believing in what cannot be seen but having the assurance of that for which we hope for will come to pass.

Have faith knowing what cannot be seen is possible. You can and will rebuild, being stronger and better.

You must move from being average to becoming exceptional. You have to move beyond the past and pain. You will build your endurance and become resilient.

If you keep your focus on the past and what used to be, you will not be able to go forward. Use the energy of the pain to refocus your mind on the new path and direction in which you need to travel.

I believe and claim that God has a plan and knows the way, and that it is our responsibility to think big, believing in and acting on our dreams.

Recall the stories of Ester, Ruth, Joseph, Moses and many others. They all suffered crises in their life and all withstood to become exceptional. All of them had to endure, persevere, and have resilience.

They were looking forward to what could be instead of focusing on that which was. If they had longed for what had been, they would never have received what God had for their future. Thus, do not long for what has passed.

Instead, eagerly embrace the new and be transformed. I say be mindful of what you put into your mind. That which you believe is what will control your actions.

James Allen stated, "As a man thinketh in his heart shall he be." King Solomon stated, "As water reflects the face so one's life reflects the heart."
~ Proverbs 27:19.

Jesus said "For the mouth speaks what the heart is full of."
~ Matthew 12:34.

In essence, what you believe of yourself flows out of your heart. Know who you are so that you can become what you are predestined to be. Speak words of light into your heart, believing in who you are. Your light will overcome the darkness.

Darkness cannot withstand light. You are a star that shines brightly and it will not be dimmed. Just as Nehemiah and Zechariah had faith in rebuilding the temple and wall thus so it shall be for each one of us. Imagine if either of them had given up, focusing on the naysayers and enemies sent to distract. They would not have rebuilt and claimed what was for them and the people of Israel. God spoke to them and they believed in His power.

This is the word of the Lord to Zerubbabel:

"Not by might nor by power, but by my Spirit,
says the Lord Almighty." ~Zechariah 4:6.

The power of this world cannot compare to the power of the Lord. Finite cannot overcome the infinite. Nothing is impossible for God. Feed your faith and know that the crises shall pass. You will withstand, coming out stronger and wiser. You will see the way, thus trust in the One who is the Way Maker and whose Word is true, never failing.

Faith over Fear

I have learned that God is in control of everything. It is not my strength or man's strength; it is God's strength. During COVID-19, I almost lost my husband, David.

My husband is asthmatic so he was vulnerable to the virus. I was so busy leaning on the understanding of man and my selfishness, that I was not leaning on God.

My husband was self-quarantined for about seven days. During this time, we had minimal contact. We were not talking much with each other.

I was so busy focusing on my feelings and selfishness, that I left my husband on his own. I was not following God's words and commands. I should have been connected to my husband, providing him with support. My selfishness made me lose focus, leading to my almost losing my husband. David was not talking, thus I left him alone, not understanding how the virus was affecting him. This attitude cost us time. I was a hypocrite.

I read the Word, sent out weekly inspirational messages to others but I was not following my own words. On the fifth day of his quarantine, I finally swallowed my pride and checked on my husband. I saw he was not getting better. In fact, he was getting worse.

His breathing was labored. He contacted his physician who prescribed an antibiotic, I rushed out to fill the prescription. After that day I stayed actively involved in his progress.

For two days, he took the medications with his condition not improving. On day seven of his self-quarantine, his breathing was so labored that he could barely not walk. It would take him 30 minutes to catch his breath.

He contacted his physician who instructed him to go to the hospital. I said okay, let's go. David said to me the most heart wrenching statement I will never forget "We can wait until you get off work at 3 pm." Mind you it was only 11 am. I almost lost it.

I told him we were going now and I immediately transported him to the hospital. Due to the virus, I could not be with him. He was on his own. I felt so alone and useless.

This goes down as one of the worst days of my life. The physicians initially tried medication that did not work.

Finally, the physician initiated the next form of treatment which would be more aggressive. The virus was trying to take over his lungs via blood clots choking off his oxygen. My husband was depressed and despondent. He kept saying he was tired.

I went into Momma Bear mode protecting her baby cub. I told him that tired was not an option. We are fighters. Jesus did not give up on the task He was given by the Father thus neither were David and I giving up.

I immediately called on the Lord for healing and redemption. I cited scripture and fasted. I called on every prayer warrior in my arsenal. I asked God for strength, mercy, grace and love.

I asked God to send his angels to the hospital, to the nurses and doctors. I asked God to be in the hospital room with my husband, I asked God for deliverance.

This was the darkest storm I have ever been through in my life. This storm has taught me multiple lessons:

- Deny self
- I am not in control, God is in control
- Lean on God all of the time for understanding and wisdom, not my understanding
- Believe in the One who is able

My faith was deeply tested. I will forever testify to the mercy and strength of the LORD. I know that He is a healer and that He answers prayers. Nothing is impossible for the LORD.

I share this story with you so that you will know in your darkest hour who to trust and who to go to. Go to the One who can do all things. In this dark time, I learned faith over fear, prayer and fasting draws you closer to God, going deeper into Him.

My husband had a dream during the virus, he called the virus Ms. Corona. One night his fever was ranging and he was in a lot of pain. Ms. Corona told him, "I got you. I am taking you with me."

David said suddenly a giant fist came through his dream and opened up. Inside of the giant fist was David. The fist said, "You can swing on him and take your best shots; however, you will not have him."

My husband was hospitalized for about 10 days before being released home and eventually recovered from the virus after two months. I am forever thankful to God for his healing. I know that faith must conquer fear.

Tornadoes

About two days before David was to be released to return home from the hospital, I had a dream about tornadoes. I had traveled to a small town and I was preparing to leave but tornadoes were approaching. For some reason I decided to ride a bike away from the storms. I was peddling down the road. All along was a small boy peddling beside me as well.

A tornado was in front and behind us causing me to detour off the road to the field, all along little boy was following me. Suddenly I jumped off my bike and grabbed the young boy with me. I laid us both down flat on the ground. I called on the name of Jesus, asking the Lord to protect me and him.

The funnel of the tornado that was in front of us was inches away from me and the young man, it passed us by not harming us. The funnel of the second tornado that had been behind was now approaching us as well. It passed inches away again from me and the young boy, again not harming us.

I told the young boy, don't move, stay flat on the ground. Once both the tornadoes had passed by and we were safe, we both got up and looked around us. There were big ditches surrounding uss; however, the ground that we had laid on was not touched. I reflected on this dream. God was speaking to me, if you trust in Me no harm will come near your tent.

If you say, "The Lord is my refuge, and you make the Most High your dwelling, no harm will overtake you, no disaster will come near your tent."
~ Psalm 91:9-10.

Believe in these words and you will withstand. God was speaking to me through this dream. He was telling me that we had endured the storm. It was not yet our time. There was more work we needed to do in his kingdom. We had soared about the storm, finding higher and better ground.

Reflection

- What is your testimony? What ways are you sharing your testimony?
- What lessons have you learned from the crises in your life?
- How is hope shown in your life?
- Which is ruling in your life, faith or fear? Based on your response, how is it being shown in your life and actions?

CHAPTER TEN

Daily Words | Pride and the Love of Money

As you progress along your journey, never forget who is responsible for all that you have and are. God will humble those who exalt themselves. Falsely thinking that you are solely responsible for your success causes you to be separated from God.

God alone is worthy and deserving of all the glory. It is because of Him that you are and I am who we are and have all that we have. Never forget to give God the glory and praise. For He is worthy all the time.

King Nebuchadnezzar had a dream that only Daniel was able to interpret. God was trying to talk to Nebuchadnezzar, giving him a warning before it was too late. He had gotten too big for his britches.

He had pumped up his head to the point that it was too heavy for his shoulders. Through the dream, God was warning Nebuchadnezzar that his kingdom was going to be taken from him, that he was going to be driven away from the people, living like a wild animal and eating grass like an ox (Daniel 3:32).

God was speaking to him; however, he was not listening. His ears and eyes were closed. During troubling times, it may take a brick upside the head to open the minds of those to which God is speaking. Well, this time it took a brick. God raised His hand and the metaphorical brick went upside Nebuchadnezzar's head to get his attention.

As Nebuchadnezzar was walking on the roof of his royal palace, he said:

> "*Is not this the great Babylon I have built as the royal residence, by my mighty power and for the glory of my majesty?*" ~ *Daniel 4:28-30.*

No sooner had his words been spoken, at the snap of the fingers, the dream was fulfilled.

Nebuchadnezzar was turned into a wild animal, and his kingdom was taken from him. At the end of the time that God had decreed, Nebuchadnezzar, raised his eyes toward heaven, and his sanity was restored.

> *He then said "I praised the Highest; I honored and glorified him who lives forever." ~ Daniel 4:34.*

Nebuchadnezzar had to be brought low to understand that God is owed and due all the glory for that which we are and have amassed. Let us never forget who our Provider is.

God gives and can take away. He gives us all for our enjoyment; however, remember that He is the one that has provided for our enjoyment. What we are and have is all due to Him. Never forget. On the pages that follow, I leave you with daily words to provide you with inspiration for your day.

Not everything will speak to you, but listen closely to the things that catch your attention, or to which you hear a still small voice. Reflect on them and let them inspire you throughout the journey of your life. Grab your wings and soar with me.

Free

God declares that he has plans to prosper and not harm us, providing each of us with hope and a future. God has stated his promise in different ways throughout His word. However, in turn we must do our part. We must seek God.

> *"You will seek me and find me when you seek me with all your heart." ~ Jeremiah 29:13.*

God desires a relationship with us. He pursues a love relationship with us. I ask, are you in turn doing the same? During times of crisis, as with the Israelites, in their darkest hours, we should be seeking God. He is our rock and our stronghold, seek and cling to Him.

"He will cover you with his feathers and under his wings you will find refuge." ~ Psalm 91:4.

When God covers us, we will not be able to see through his wings. Know that we do not need to see, just trust in HIM. The key word is trust. We cannot please God without faith, and we can't develop faith without trusting Him.

Seek shelter and solace from the One who is able thus there is no need to worry or be anxious. God will deliver and provide.

That which we allow to place our mind in bondage we must release. We cannot stop a bird from flying over our head but we can prevent the bird from building a nest in our mind. We can't stop other people from gossiping and talking about us, but we can stop letting their words weigh upon our mind. We can dwell on God's word, not people's.

Apply this concept of choice to the storms and trials in your life. The storm is present; you might not be able to see the light above you; however, you cannot allow the storm to build a nest of fear or anxiousness in your head. Your mind is yours alone. Focus your mind on that which will release you to be free which is the Lord.

"You will keep in perfect peace those whose minds are steadfast, because they trust in you." ~ Isaiah 26:3.

Let Go

You must let go of what you believe you are to embrace who God needs you to become what He knows you are. Prior to Saul's becoming the Apostle Paul, he was the ringleader in persecuting the disciples, until he had an encounter with God that changed his life. Due to his encounter with God, he became who he was created to be, accepting, embracing, and fulfilling his assignment. Each of us must evolve and grow to answer and accept God's call. Jesus says it best.

"Whoever wants to be my disciple must deny themselves and take up their cross and follow me." ~ Matthew 16:24.

Say No to Complacency

Complacency does not lead to change. Look at the issues we face daily in this world. There has been no change or progression. The root cause is complacency.

Complacency promotes mediocrity and settling for the status quo. If the lepers in 2 King 7 had not taken action they would have died. Instead, they chose to go outside of their comfort zone leading to their being healed. In life we must take action, standing still is not an option.

In the same way:

"Faith by itself, if not accompanied by action, is dead." ~ *James 2:17.*

Can't is Not an Option

Why is it so easy for us to use the words can't and won't? These words block and hinder us from reaching our potential. In essence, we are convincing ourselves that being below average and average is acceptable. We settle for less than we could have in our lives. This should never be acceptable. In the *Last Dance*, Michael Jordan showed us that he became great because being the best was not an option. Each of us must do the same to become better.

Each day, we should strive to be better than yesterday. The Apostle Paul said it best. He told his readers that in a race all runners run, but only one gets the prize. Each of us needs to run our race to get the prize.

In life, each of us has a prize waiting in heaven. The prize is the realization of your why and unleashing all that is within you. Remove the words can't and won't from your vocabulary. Focus on becoming better each day of your life.

Get Out of the Way

What is stopping you from moving forward? What is holding you back? I say it is you. You must believe and have faith in self.

You and I have all that we need within to become, realizing our dreams and unleashing our potential.

Faith in yourself and that which is within you will allow you to soar to new heights and limits. Believe in that which is within you. You have gifts and talents that will lead to your realizing your dreams. We must stop being our own roadblocks instead of making the turn leading to opportunities and growth.

Not Silver and Gold

You do not need silver and gold because you have faith in the name of Jesus.

Faith in Jesus can and will make all possible that appear impossible. Stop focusing on materialistic things that you can see, and instead focus on your spiritual resources, that which is within you, what you cannot see.

In Acts 3, a lame beggar who encountered the disciples was seeking gold or silver. They told him they had no money, but would give him what they had — healing.

The healing he received was worth more than gold. This same principle applies to us. Look within yourself and that which is within you because you have all you need and much more. You can do all that you seek with faith.

Chose Courage

"Today I will focus on courage." What does that affirmation mean to you? Are you showing focus in your life? Do you have faith in God's Word and yourself?

When the Apostle Paul was headed to stand trial before Caesar, the ship he was traveling in faced a great storm. The men on the ship were scared and lost hope; however, Paul did not.

Paul said "So keep your courage, men, for I have faith in God that it will happen just as He told me." ~ Acts 27:25.

When God talks to you do you keep the faith and have courage? Or do you get angry or depressed and begin to doubt the plans God has for your life?

"Better" Requires Sacrifice

Each of us has dreams and aspirations to become better. I ask how much are you willing to sacrifice and suffer to achieve what you desire. With achievement and success comes sacrifice and hard work.

Our failures are lessons that become the building blocks to our success. How far are you willing to be stretched? Are you all in?

God said to Abraham, *"From you I will make a great nation."* However, to receive this promise, Abraham had to leave all he had behind and travel to a foreign country. He had no home; however, he was all in and believed.

"By faith Abraham, when called to go to a place he would later receive as his inheritance, obeyed and went, even though he did not know where he was going." ~ Hebrews 11:8.

God knows the way. He's seen our lives from beginning to end. We just need to trust and follow Him when He calls.

What is Your Fragrance?

Do you know how perfume is made? The flowers must first be crushed, and ground up before they can be used. They don't release their sweet scent until they are crushed and broken.

Only after being crushed are they ready to be made into perfume and other fragrances. Is your being crushed right now releasing a pleasant aroma or a stink?

Did you know that garlic is one of the ingredients that almost always needs to be minced, chopped or crushed before using it in a recipe? It's a rare recipe that calls for whole cloves of garlic. When we cut into an onion, or crush a clove of garlic, or chop up herbs for a meal, that's when they release the flavors and scents we love so much to taste or smell. God has gifted us with his Spirit to spread the aroma of life, lifting up and being a light in this dark world. Your fragrance should be pleasing and sweet not bitter.

Each of us are representatives of the Lord, assisting in bringing others into the light.

"For we are to God the pleasing aroma of Christ among those who are being saved and those who are perishing." ~ 2 Corinthians 2:15.

Check your fragrance. Your fragrance should be attractive, pulling people into Christ's love, not chasing them away.

Molding Character to Match Assignment

I ask that you join me in meditating on God developing our character to match our assignment. Many times, we seek to be removed from our circumstances; however, God keeps us where we are because we are not ready.

He has not promised to remove us *from* our situation, but He has promised to be with us *through* our situation. He could have lifted Shadrach, Meshach, and Abednego from the fire, but instead He walked with them through it.

We cannot be given our assignment until we have been prepared. Reflect on your circumstances and think upon how you have grown because of where you are.

You have been pruned because God is building your character. When we have trees, shrubs, or bushes or vegetable plants we prune them to ensure they become stronger and produce more fruit or flowers.

You aren't being punished because you're going through tough times. You're being pruned because God wants to see more from you! The Lord directs your steps, not you.

"Lord, I know that people's lives are not their own; it is not for them to direct their steps." ~ Jeremiah 10:23.

What is Your Why?

Your purpose is connected to your why. Your why is why you were created. What is it that you need to be doing that will add value to yourself, others and your community? This week meditate on your why.

What work is God doing around you that you should be involved with and assisting in? Once you have determined what your why is, God will provide the rest.

"It is God who works in you to will and to act according to his good purpose." ~ Philippians 2:13.

We will not live forever so it is imperative that we embrace our cause and our why, running the race for which we have been predestined. Our goal is to finish well. We do not wish to look back with regrets so we must seize our opportunities and possibilities. Even if no one else is watching you, or seeing your progress, God knows. He is waiting at the finish line for each one of us.

The Apostle Paul says it best. "I consider my life worth nothing to me, my only aim is to finish the race." ~ Acts 20:24.

Are you running your race? More importantly, are you running it to win?

Created to Soar

What is your focus today and for this week? Each day you must seek to be intentional, adding value to yourself and focusing on becoming better.

One week my pastor's message included an analogy about eagles. In storms eagles don't stop flying. They go higher seeking better, calmer winds and going above the storm. This same principle applies to each of us. There may be times when the storm is raging around us and we are in the calm of the eye of the storm, but dreading the storm around us. This does not mean we stop soaring. We have options in a crisis which are opportunities. We must determine the course of action. We must choose to soar, finding higher ground leading to evolving and growing.

"They will soar on wings like eagles; they will run and not grow weary; they will walk and not be faint." ~ Isaiah 40:41.

Focus on soaring as you were created to do.

ABOUT THE AUTHOR

For over 20 years I held various leadership positions in companies and organizations.

I have learned that leadership is not based on title. Leadership is based on influence. I saw the need to help build up and add value to others, sparking me to become a speaker, trainer, coach and author. I provide training on Leadership, Communication, Team Building, Connecting and Attitude.

Prior to launching my business, Faith Hope & Spirit, LLC, I was discontent and distressed, resulting in my being distracted and unfulfilled.

I was a person without a cause, a purpose. Around me were people who were in leadership positions; however, who were not leaders. They were merely people taking a walk because no one was following.

Because of them, I realized that this world is lacking our values and beliefs. We must change our mindset, becoming positive and consistent.

Thus, I found my why. I undertook the journey to develop my plan of action, being committed as a change agent. I sought to change my world and thus the experiences of those around me.

The spark for me was a course I stumbled upon in my Church, Discipleship 101. The instructor would constantly ask the question - Are you ready to answer the call? Are you prepared?

I have always valued self, I looked in my mirror seeing value and worth. As I value myself I seek to add value to others. Being a servant matters most to me. Thus, the instructor's question inspired me to write my first two books *Reflections from Within* and *Messages from the Spirit.*

My mission is to sharpen others. I am passionate about partnering with individuals and teams developing a commitment to growing and learning resulting in changing their world and those around them.

As we grow, we foster change and spread hope. We must believe and have faith in what can be and not become complacent with that which is.

BEFORE YOU GO

If you have enjoyed this book, or have been inspired by it, please consider leaving a review on Amazon, or telling a friend or family member about this book.

God's words come alive and move in people's lives when we pray, meditate and most importantly when we share our insights and inspiration with others.

If there is a sister, coworker, parent, spouse, brother, or friend in your life who you think could benefit or be inspired by this book, please take time to tell them about it, and about what you liked about it.

I pray that you too are inspired to trust God and see that the challenges or what looks like chaos and trouble happening in your life isn't random, or bad luck. The things you're going through right now are part of God's plan for your life. If you're not a believer, God may be trying to get your attention so you accept and trust Him and His plan for your life.

Trust God and ask Him to show you what He's trying to teach you. And, if you aren't a believer in Jesus Christ, or haven't made up your mind about Him, or if God is real, I assure you, He is! And He loves you!

God has a plan for your life too. If you want to know how to ask God into your life, and experience the love and abundance, and eternal life He offers, just give Him your life. It's not hard and it will make a huge difference in your life and in your eternity.

How to Become A Christian

When a Roman soldier asked the Apostle Paul how to become saved, (Acts 16:30-31), Paul answered, *"Believe on the Lord Jesus Christ and you will be saved. If you confess with your mouth 'Jesus is Lord' and believe in your heart that God raised him from the dead, you will be saved.*

For it with your heart that you believe and are justified, and it is with your mouth that you confess and are saved." (Romans 10:9-10)

"For whosoever shall call upon the name of the Lord shall be saved." (Romans 10:13)

The ABC's of becoming saved:

Here is a simple 3-step process to accepting Jesus as Savior.

- A—Admit *that I am a sinner (Romans 3:23, Romans 6:23).*
- B—Believe *that Jesus is God's Son, that He died for me, and that His death can save my soul (John 3:16, Romans 5:8-10).*
- C—Confess *that He is my Lord and Savior (Romans 10:9-13).*

Your decision regarding your salvation is the most important prayer you will ever say. It will define your entire life here on earth, but more importantly, it will assure you eternity in heaven.

When you sincerely pray this prayer and ask Christ into your life; you will never be the same. You will have a purpose for living and a Person (Christ) to live for. Your prayer doesn't have to be long or complicated. Personalize it however feels right for you:

Dear God, I admit I am a sinner and I understand that Jesus died on the cross for my sins. I believe that Jesus Christ is your son, that He came to earth, lived a perfect life and died on the cross to pay the price for my sins. Please forgive me for all my sins and come into my heart. I want to follow You for the rest of my life. In Jesus' Name, Amen.

If you prayed this prayer, or one like it, Welcome to the Family of God and an eternity in heaven.

Once you accept Christ into your heart, begin reading the Bible. Start with the book of John, or any of the four gospels — Matthew, Mark, Luke, or John.

Find a church and share your prayer with the minister. Some people feel lighter and happier after praying the prayer, some feel nothing at all. I assure you if you start trusting God, read your Bible, and find other believers to talk to about God, you'll see and feel a difference.

www.ingramcontent.com/pod-product-compliance
Lightning Source LLC
Chambersburg PA
CBHW050900180626
46814CB00007B/2819